The Shooters

Illustrated by Oliver Chadwick

Rebecca, captain of Springholm Shooters
Netball Team, has several problems to sort
out if they are to win the Manor House cup,
and not all of them are concerned with playing
skills and tactics . . .

The practice match with the local boys'
basketball team turns out to be not so much a
friendly match as a test of survival, especially
for Keeley, a girl who desperately wants to be
a success.

MICHAEL HARDCASTLE

The Shooters

A Magnet Book

Also by Michael Hardcastle
in Magnet Books

Away from Home
Caught Out
Fast from the Gate
Free Kick
Half a Team
In the Net
Roar to Victory
The Saturday Horse
Soccer Special
The Switch Horse
The Team That Wouldn't Give In
Tiger of the Track
United!
Winning Rider

First published in 1986
by Methuen Children's Books Ltd
This Magnet paperback edition first published 1988
by Methuen Children's Books Ltd
A Division of OPG Services Limited
Michelin House, 81 Fulham Road, London SW3 6RB
Reprinted 1988
Text copyright © 1986 Michael Hardcastle
Illustrations copyright © 1986 Oliver Chadwick
Printed in Great Britain by
Cox & Wyman Ltd, Reading

ISBN 0 416 07512 6

One

Rebecca cleared a space on the steamed-up mirror with the sleeve of her tracksuit and peered briefly at herself. Her auburn hair was damp but presentable and she didn't *look* tired. All the same, she hadn't felt at her best this evening. There'd been no sparkle in her play. Of course, that could be because she was missing Julie. When Julie wasn't in the team, the game was never quite so enjoyable.

As she slowly left the changing-room she could hear a ball being bounced against a wall. So one player, at least, was still on the court. Rebecca didn't need to catch sight of her to know that it would be Keeley Hilton. For some unknown reason, Keeley had got it into her head that she had to practise every minute she could steal from the day or the night.

'Going home *already*?' Keeley remarked disappointedly as Rebecca crossed the corner of the court.

'Well, I don't usually have a shower and then *start* playing, you know,' Rebecca replied mildly. As captain of the team, she didn't believe in using sarcasm on her players: but, from time to time, she forgot her own rules.

'But I need a partner, someone to practise with, just for a bit,' Keeley pleaded. 'And everybody else has just pushed off.'

'Look, I'm not going through all that routine again, not for anybody,' Rebecca said with just a hint of exasperation in her voice. 'Frankly, I've done enough training for an entire week, let alone one night.'

'But it's all right for you,' Keeley objected. 'I mean, you're a natural games player. You've got an instinct for putting the ball through the net. It's no effort for you, is it, Rebecca? I've got to work like mad to reach a good standard. I've even got to work like mad just to keep my weight down. Not like some. . . .'

She didn't have to add that weight was not a problem for Rebecca. Often, when she had to give her name in full, she would say, 'I'm Rebecca Westmoreland – and yes, I know, I'm as long as my name. And thin with it.' Her height, though, was one of her greatest assets as a netball player. As Springholm Shooters' Goal-shooter she had a towering advantage over all her team-mates: and, indeed, over the majority of girls of her age. Now she gave Keeley a speculative look.

'You're really getting quite keen, Kee, aren't you?' she remarked with an air of slight surprise. 'What's turned you on to netball so suddenly?'

Keeley didn't answer immediately. She appeared to be looking over Rebecca's shoulder as if seeking inspiration.

'Well,' she said eventually, when Rebecca didn't prompt her further, 'I want to achieve something. I'd like to be – well – in a winning team. I think you'll win something, the way you lead the side, the way you and Julie keep scoring. Like clockwork it is sometimes. I want to be part of the success.'

This time Rebecca's surprise was obvious.

'But why netball? I mean, I always thought hockey was your game. You're pretty good at that. You and Sandra used to be practically as thick as a cheese sandwich. Oh, sorry! I don't mean that in a, er, physical sense, Kee. It's just a phrase my uncle uses. Sort of family expression.'

Keeley's smile was wan.

'It's all right, Rebecca, I'm not offended. I don't see much of Sandra these days. In fact, I can't stand the sight of her. Anyway, I've gone off hockey. Not a very civilised game. No style, you know. Netball –

well, netball's skilful. *And* it's good for the figure. All that running and jumping and twisting. At hockey you can be out of the action for minutes on end. Well, it seems like that, anyway.'

Rebecca raised her eyebrows and tightened her lips. But she didn't voice the questions she immediately wanted to ask. In any case, she doubted that Keeley would answer them: answer them truthfully, anyway.

'Well,' she said instead, drawing the words out like a piece of elastic, 'we haven't really decided on our best team yet. I mean, Tara is desperate to keep the Centre spot – and I think she definitely has the edge on you at the moment, Keeley. Sorry to be so blunt but, well, there's no point in being dishonest, is there?'

Keeley swallowed and shook her head.

'Yeah, I suppose so,' she agreed, only half reluctantly. 'But, you see, Rebecca, that's why I need to practise more, all the time. That's why I could do with a bit more coaching.'

Rebecca wasn't going to give way on that.

'Well, you could always join another team playing in a different league,' she suggested. 'You know what Julie's like, playing non-stop for goodness knows how many teams all the time. Don't know where she gets all her energy from. I expect she could fix you up with another team that's rather short of players.'

'I don't think Julie likes me very much,' Keeley admitted in a low voice. 'I think she feels I don't try hard enough. But I do, honestly I do! I can't convince her, though. I'm thankful you're the captain and not Julie. I mean, I know that you and she are the best of friends but you're quite different about how you treat people. Julie doesn't want to know anybody she thinks is, well, an *inferior* player.'

Rebecca sighed. Instinctively, she glanced at Keeley's reddish hair. People who automatically associated that shade with an aggressive personality had certainly got it wrong so far as Keeley was concerned. She was a pleader, a whiner almost, in Rebecca's view. There was nothing belligerent about her outlook on life.

'You do seem a bit, well, *unlucky* with people at present, don't you?' Rebecca said with some sympathy. 'I mean, you've fallen out with Sandra and you don't get on with Julie. I understand that, in a way, but netball's such a *team* game. People have got to get on with each other. I know it's a bit of a cliché to say it nowadays but team spirit really is very important.'

'Oh yes, I know it is!' Keeley was anxious not to be misunderstood. The last person she wanted to fall

out with was Rebecca. In her eyes, Rebecca was someone to be admired for all manner of reasons. 'Truly I haven't fallen out with Julie. I like her a lot. I think she's a terrific player. It's just that I'm not good enough to *impress* her yet. That's why I'm so keen to improve my play, Rebecca.'

Rebecca nodded and half-turned towards the exit as if to indicate that it was time to leave.

'O.K., well I'll have a word with Julie myself. We

need a strong squad if we're going to win a trophy this season. Julie seems to think we'll be the best in the league but I'm not so sure. A couple of injuries to key players can knock your chances right on the head however good the team is.'

Keeley didn't want her to leave. She didn't, however, know how to detain her. The last thing she wanted was to be considered 'clinging'. Rebecca, she sensed, was a bit of a loner, in spite of her friendship with Julie and, to a lesser degree, the rest of the team she captained. She belonged to several organisations and clubs but it appeared that she didn't share her interests with the same people all the time. Most of the time, she went her own way.

'Are you walking home or is anybody picking you up?' Keeley asked.

Rebecca hesitated. 'Er, not exactly. I mean, I'm walking home but I'm not going straight there. I said I'd drop in and have a word with Kathy Hayman. She runs the Red Cross Youth and I, well, I help her out with the training programme, you know.'

'No,' Keely said quickly, 'I didn't know, Rebecca. You're a member, are you?'

Rebecca nodded. 'Have been since I was, oh, quite tiny, really. It's got lots of interesting – well, fascinating – aspects that people don't know much about. Like survival training and accident prevention and community help. All sorts of things. Plus raising money in different ways.'

'Oh, great,' said Keeley, hoping to hear more.

Rebecca, though, looked at her watch again. She didn't want to deflate Keeley but, equally, she felt the need to be on her own for a time. A compromise was needed.

'Look, I'm going down Clifford Road so why don't you walk that way with me and then you can cut off home across Rising Fields?' she suggested.

'Oh, fine, thanks very much, Rebecca!'

It was obvious to Rebecca that the other girl really was delighted to be shown such consideration. She couldn't help wondering what on earth had gone wrong between Keeley and Sandra for the break to be so complete. Perhaps, one of these days, she'd be told the reason.

They chatted, on the way, about nothing of importance: about school, about clothes, about pets (Keeley had a rabbit, of which she was plainly very fond. It seemed to Rebecca that a rabbit was just the sort of pet a girl like Keeley would choose, but she didn't say so). Both of them would have preferred to discuss netball but each thought the other wanted to avoid the subject.

When they reached Jubilee Hall Keeley didn't

12

simply say 'Cheerio' and go off on her own. She seemed to be waiting for an invitation. Rebecca sighed inwardly.

'Look, I'd invite you in, Kee, but I'm sure you'd be bored to death. I mean I'll just be discussing things with Kathy, so –'

'No, I wouldn't be bored, Rebecca! Definitely not. I really would just like to know more about, well, whatever the Red Cross does.'

Rebecca suppressed a shrug.

'O.K., then,' she said resignedly. 'Come on in, then.'

Two

Keeley tended to hang back as she followed Rebecca into the building, almost as if she were fearful of meeting someone she wouldn't like. Then they both had to stand aside by the inner door to allow a rather excited group of younger girls to come through. All were wearing heavy duty navy blue sweaters with a Red Cross badge on each sleeve.

Nearly every one of them greeted Rebecca cheerfully and some inquired if she'd had a good game that evening. Keeley noticed how politely Rebecca replied to them, nearly always using their name, however brief the exchange. That courtesy, that consideration for others, was something Keeley had always been aware of in Rebecca's captaincy. It impressed her deeply. She wished Julie, for one, would adopt that attitude.

'Hi, Natalie. Have you been enjoying yourself?'

Rebecca was talking to a small girl with a face as

14

round as a ball. Natalie used her forefinger like a scraper to rub her nose.

'Well, we played a game to get us to learn the phonetic alphabet but I'm not very good at that.'

Keeley's frown was noticed by Rebecca. 'Alpha, Bravo, Charlie, Delta, Echo – you know, communicating by initial letters,' she explained.

'Oh,' said Keeley, not realising such things were part of an organisation like the Red Cross. 'What's – oh, W?'

'Whiskey,' Rebecca replied with a laugh.

'I can *never* get that far down – I can only go as far as M for Mike,' complained Natalie. 'It's too hard, Becky.'

'That's because you stick to repeating the easy bits at the beginning, Natalie. You've got to start *half-way* and keep repeating it from there. Then you'll get it into your head. Begin at November and Oscar and Papa – they're good ones. Before you know what's happening you'll find you've cracked it.'

Natalie scratched her dimpled chin as well as her nose this time and then said she'd have to go. Mum got cross if she turned up late every night.

'You mean Mike Uniform Mike, don't you?' Rebecca joked as they said good-bye.

'Natalie can't wait to start looking after babies,'

Rebecca told Keeley. 'Funny, isn't it, she seems hardly more than a baby herself, when you think of her size. But she's already decided she's destined to be a nurse. Well, not just any nurse, one of the world's *great* nurses!'

'Do you get a lot of training, then, in how to treat injuries? Is that what it's all about?'

'Well, certainly, that's a very big part of what we do. After all, the Red Cross was actually founded to assist wounded soldiers on the battlefield. So practical first aid and coping with casualties is very important to us. Oh, and that means knowing about the human body and how to care for it. Child care and nursing are all part of that – and, of course, those are the bits girls like Natalie love.'

'What about you, Rebecca? What do you like best?'

Rebecca didn't reply immediately. She pondered the matter as they crossed the large hall with its stage at the far end. 'Well, I like it all, really. I like the organising bit very –'

She was interrupted by a tall, angular woman striding briskly towards them and wearing the uniform sweater with a rainbow of badges on her arm. It was quite evident that she really was very pleased to see Rebecca; but she also immediately took an interest in Rebecca's companion.

Rebecca introduced her as Kathy Hayman, who ran their section of Red Cross Youth. 'And this is Keeley Hilton, who plays in our netball team.'

Hands were shaken in a rather formal manner and then Mrs Hayman, with eyebrows raised, asked whether Keeley was to be a new recruit.

'Er, well, that wasn't exactly the idea,' Rebecca said, looking a trifle embarrassed. 'She just came in with me because, er, well because we were together.'

'Oh, but I am interested, *very* interested,' Keeley cut in quickly, not wanting to be excluded.

'Well, if that's the case then you've got the best person to tell you what we get up to,' was Mrs Hayman's smooth response. 'Rebecca, I always tell everyone, is my right hand – invaluable in helping with *everything* that we do. But if I could just take her away for a moment – something we must decide on without delay....'

While the two of them withdrew to a small room behind the stage Keeley wandered around the hall, studying posters and achievement graphs. She was quite content to be on her own, knowing that Rebecca would soon rejoin her, even if only for a few minutes. She guessed that Springholm's skipper hadn't intended to invite her to join the Red Cross; but if ever she did Keeley thought she would accept. It wasn't that she was particularly keen on learning about child health or forms of communication for use in emergencies; but the social aspects of such a group were appealing. Even if she were a suitable candidate for such an organisation, however, she suspected that first she'd have to gain Rebecca's support or at least approval.

Genuine friendship was something she wouldn't be able to count on – yet.

'Sorry I got dragged away,' Rebecca apologised as she rejoined her team-mate a few minutes later. 'But she wanted to make sure I knew what materials we were going to use to make up the casualties.'

'Make up casualties! What do you mean – put lipstick and eye shadow and that sort of stuff on them?' She was truly amazed.

Rebecca laughed. 'No, of course not! Honestly, Keeley, I thought you'd have guessed what I mean. I'm talking about dummies – the life-like figures we use for demonstration purposes. To show people how to handle patients and how to apply a tourniquet and bandages and splints and so on. I have to prepare some of these dummies, casualties, for an exhibition.'

'Oh, sorry.' Keeley felt thoroughly foolish 'Er, do you do a lot of those sort of jobs on your own – you know, making preparations for demonstrations and things?'

Rebecca hunched her shoulders. 'Well, sometimes. Kathy Hayman seems to regard me as her second-in-command or something. So she tends to ask me to get on with things when she herself has to be away for any reason. She's a top architect and sometimes she has to go off to London for a few days, usually at a highly inconvenient time for us, or so she always claims.'

'Obviously she thinks pretty highly of you.'

This time Rebecca's laugh contained a hint of embarrassment. 'Yes, Kathy does lay it on a bit thick, I must say. Wish she wouldn't.'

They moved, in step, towards the door and it was only then that Keeley realised Rebecca was ready to leave. She had supposed they would be there for some time, half-an-hour at least. She felt a surge of disappointment.

'Is Julie a Red Cross member?' Keeley inquired.

'Good heavens, no. What made you think that?'

'Well, you two always seem to be pretty close, so, well, I thought –'

'No, no. When we're not playing netball she goes her way and I go mine. Julie spends all her spare time, as far as I can judge, playing more netball and various other sports. I haven't her energy. I think that one of these days she'll overdo it. But you try telling her that.'

They reached the street. Rebecca started to say something and then stopped. She had been thinking about inviting Keeley to come along to the next Red Cross meeting, just as a kindly gesture. But if she did, she had a feeling that Keeley would build an entire friendship on it.

'See you at the match against Netherlee on Tuesday then,' she said brightly. She should have foreseen what Keeley's reaction would be.

'Will I be in the team, do you think? I mean, er, will I be *considered* for a place?'

20

Rebecca was thankful the stocky girl had added the second sentence. It meant she didn't have to hand out instant disappointment.

'Oh yes, I'm sure you'll be in the running for a place, Kee,' she said as cheerfully as possible. 'But nothing will be decided until that evening, until Julie and I have had a chance to sort out one or two things. I mean, you never know who might not turn up, who might be sick or something.'

'True,' agreed Keeley, brightening too. 'So long as I'm present I'm in with a chance of playing. Thanks, Rebecca, that's great. I promise I'll not let you down.'

'Fine,' Rebecca answered casually. 'So long, then.'

As she headed for home, however, Rebecca couldn't help wondering whether she had made a mistake in encouraging Keeley to think she might win a place in the team. She sensed that Keeley might not be able to withstand another rejection if she were excluded.

Three

The match against Netherlee was a Cup-tie and when the draw was made Julie France had immediately voiced her contempt for the opposition.

'Netherlee are *pathetic*,' she told Rebecca. 'Absolutely pathetic. Honestly, we ought not to be forced to play such a feeble team. I mean, look at their record: bottom of the lowest division in the League, hardly any goals scored and a terrible record of goals against.'

'Well, at least we should be able to win easily,' was Rebecca's mild reply. 'That can't be bad.'

'Yes it can!' Julie shot back. 'A team improves by playing good teams, teams better than themselves if possible. The competition sharpens you up. With poor opposition you can get sloppy and complacent. That's not good for morale. And if you do win easily you can think you're better than you really are.'

There were times, and this was one of them, when Rebecca felt that it was Julie, not herself, who should be captaining Springholm Shooters. She possessed much more tactical awareness of the game than Rebecca and was forever thinking about overall strategy for the team and how players could improve their individual skills. Rebecca recognised that she herself tended to lead simply by instinct (and, sometimes, she knew, by inspiration). Yet Julie had no wish at all to be captain: she claimed that if she had to think of, and for, others all the time then her own game, and skills, would suffer.

Now, on the evening of the game itself, Julie was still of the opinion that the match with Netherlee would be a waste of time. She had almost decided against turning up to play, she told Rebecca as they walked towards the changing-room.

'Well, you don't have to play even now if you don't want to,' Rebecca pointed out. 'I mean, we can easily switch the team around and put Karen in your place as Goal-attack. You know she always wants a change from being Goalkeeper!'

Julie wrinkled her nose at that suggestion but didn't make any verbal comment.

'And then,' Rebecca went on, 'we can give a bit of experience to a couple of other players, like Keeley Hilton and Louise Peckett. I know that Keeley is

23

desperate to make a good impression and get into the team on a regular basis.'

This time Julie actually snorted. 'Keeley! Keeley's not good enough for our team, not by a street. She's just – well, slow is the kindest thing to say. She's a pudding, a Christmas pudding. Quite good to look at but heavy on the, er, system. Hey, that's not bad, Becky, is it?'

'It's not fair, not by a long way,' her friend replied sharply. 'I had a good talk with her last week and I know how keen she is to do well. She's putting in a lot of extra training and wants to play for us. Julie, she really is very enthusiastic. We should give her a chance.'

'Enthusiasm's O.K. but it doesn't make up for lack of skill – or speed. *La* Hilton can't change that just by doing catching practice and trying a few sprints.'

By now they were at the entrance to the changing-room and Rebecca could think of no argument she could use in Keeley's favour: everything Julie had said couldn't really be challenged.

They always arrived ahead of everyone else, though that was by instinct, not prior arrangement; neither of them had ever mentioned to the other that this was what they should do. It was very much like their partnership in the team: on the court each could sense where the other was and whether she was well placed to take a pass. For once, however, someone had arrived ahead of them. Hanging on one of the pegs was a track suit and, below the bench, was a pair of blue shoes.

'Who on earth's that?' Julie asked, totally astonished.

She didn't wait for an answer but reached for the track suit top and turned it inside out to check if there was a name tab. There was and it read: Keeley Hilton.

'She must be out on the court, or running around somewhere close by,' Julie said wonderingly. 'I see what you mean by being keen, but –'

'Look, we could give her a chance,' Rebecca cut in, seizing her opportunity. 'If Netherlee are as bad as you think they are and we're going to win easily then I'm quite willing to let Keeley go on in my place. If necessary, we can substitute her at half-time and I'll be back in the team. You can be skipper for once – do you good to run things, Julie!'

'No, I've got a better idea,' Julie replied emphatically. '*La* Hilton can take *my* place from the start. Then if she's no good at all we'll call her off by saying she's injured. We'll warn her –'

'Oh no!' Rebecca was horror-struck at such a suggestion. 'We're not having players feigning injury and being taken off. That's breaking the rules of the game and I don't believe in that kind of attitude. I didn't think you did, either.'

Julie shrugged expressively.

'We wouldn't be doing anything other teams don't do at some stage of the season,' she pointed out. 'In any case, we don't need to pull any tricks to beat Netherlee. As I've said before, we could defeat them with only five players if we had to! Look, let's see what Keeley is up to. If I think she's improved then she can definitely take my place – well, until half-time, anyway. I could do with a rest, Becky.'

'I was thinking earlier you looked a bit, well, jaded,' her friend admitted. 'Were you playing last night as well or something?'

'Actually, I played a couple of games. One for a school team I'm supposed to be helping out and they were short of a player. Oh, and then I turned out for Loxford Ladies – super team in the making, Becky. Won easily – I scored twenty. Honestly, I ought to get you to join them, too. We'd be a great hit with them.'

Rebecca didn't respond to that. She and Julie had always been candid with each other about everything and that didn't stop short of personal comments.

'No wonder,' she said in a matter-of-fact tone,

'you look worn out tonight – well, half-worn out, anyway. You can't play as often as that and still feel fresh and ready-to-go for the next match. Impossible. Julie, you've got to cut out some of these other games or you'll be on your knees. You're not being fair to Springholm, either, are you?'

'I've told you, I'll get by,' Julie answered, frowning. 'Look, let's go and see the Hilton in action, see if she's as capable as you think. You know me, I wouldn't let the team down. I'd die for it! So there!'

That, Rebecca knew, was true: or it was when Julie said it. Later events often caused her to go back on her word in spite of her protestations that she didn't do such things. Part of the truth about Julie France was that she always meant well but wasn't always able to do well.

Even before they stepped on to the outdoor court they spotted Keeley, practising shooting, something Rebecca wouldn't have expected of her. After all, the role Keeley wanted was Centre, not Goal-shooter or Goal-attack. But, neatly and effectively, she flipped the ball through the ring and then backed away for a shot from a different distance, a different angle.

'I can see she really has got her sights set on my place,' Julie commented drily. 'If she goes on like

that I shall soon feel quite redundant.'

Before Rebecca could explain that she was as surprised as Julie, Keeley put the ball down and began to do a series of squat thrusts, a fitness exercise that Rebecca greatly favoured for training purposes. It was also the sort of routine that would benefit anyone carrying a bit too much weight, especially on the thighs.

Keeley hadn't spotted their presence. She gave herself minimal rest after completing a notably long sequence of thrusts before switching to jumping on the spot, her knees pulled high as possible on every

28

leap. It was quite an impressive performance.

'Well, that's it then,' Julie declared decisively. '*La* Hilton takes my place in the first half and we'll see how she gets on. If she turns out to be sensationally successful then you can keep her there for the whole match. You never know, Becky: this could be the most inspired bit of team selection of your entire career!'

Rebecca wasn't sure now what she should do. It was obvious Julie would welcome a break; and that Keeley's own enthusiasm and determination to succeed might make her into a useful, if not outstanding, replacement. And, as all the Spring holm players knew from their encounter the previous season, Netherlee were a poor team. The Shooters should be capable of defeating them even if playing at no more than half speed. But –

'O.K.,' she agreed suddenly. She had glimpsed the arrival of other members of the team. 'I'll do it.'

Before she could change her mind she called out to Keeley, who looked surprised to have been spotted. She came over to her captain and Julie, smiled affably – and then her jaw literally dropped.

'You're joking, aren't you?' she gasped, looking from Rebecca to the girl she'd been told she was to replace. '*Please* don't tease me, Rebecca. My nerves won't stand it!'

She paused. Then, when neither of the other girls uttered a word but just continued to smile at her, she began to accept that it must be true after all.

'I'm really going to play in this Cup-tie – and I'm really going to be Goal-attack?' she murmured. 'Wow! And – again – WOW!'

'So you'd better be good, or I'll claim my place back again,' Julie told her. 'Oh, yes, and if you get a scissors-like signal from me that'll mean you're to start limping and say you've knocked your knee or turned your ankle or something, so –'

'Julie!' Rebecca cut in.

'– you'll have to come off and I can go on as substitute,' Julie continued without pause. 'I mean, it'll be just a strategic move, Keeley, in the team's interests. O.K.? So keep your eye on me. Becky will be too busy to give the message herself.'

Rebecca sighed heavily to express her disapproval. But she realised it wasn't going to help matters by countermanding Julie's instructions. Anyway, Keeley would suppose that she (Rebecca) and Julie had worked out this ploy between them. Everyone seemed to believe that Rebecca and Julie were of the same mind about everything.

'Yeah, whatever you say,' Keeley agreed breathlessly. All she could think about was that she was in the team for the start of the match. How long she stayed on court was less important in her mind.

Karen Honley, Springholm's Goalkeeper, came on to the court with two of the other players; all three were already dressed in the Shooters' scarlet skirt and lime-green blouse. Spectators and other teams often commented on the colour combination but Springholm were proud of their outfit. Rebecca believed that a team that looked good usually felt good and thus played well. So far the theory was working because Springholm were having a good season. They were, Julie reckoned, just short of one other class player, either at Centre or Wing-attack. Until they found such a player it was unlikely they would win the League or even finish runners-up. However, as Karen had pointed out more than once, the Cup was a great leveller and so it represented their best chance of picking up a trophy that season. It was Karen's dearest wish to win a medal or replica to put in the display cabinet in the family's sitting-room. Most of the space on the shelves was occupied by the plaques and cups and medals awarded to her brother, a demon squash player. She thought it was time someone else in the family claimed a little of the public glory that went with sporting success.

'Hey, Kee, come and try to beat me,' Karen called.

She was, inevitably, tall; and her ash-blonde, shoulder-length hair always attracted a lot of attention from spectators. Karen was well aware of her good looks and sometimes was tempted to be a show-off.

Obediently Keeley crossed to the shooting circle where she received a fierce pass from Zoe Ablett, Karen's partner in defence. Instinctively, Keeley ducked, weaved, stepped back a pace and then very accurately flicked the ball out of Karen's reach and through the goal.

'Huh, beginner's luck!' Karen laughed. 'You won't do that to me again in a month of matches.'

'I don't care as long as I do it against Netherlee's Goalkeeper just as soon as we get started,' Keeley told her with a dazzling smile.

'No chance of that! You'll never get on the court.'

'You're completely out of date, Karen! I'm in the team from the *start*. *And* I'm taking Julie's place. I'm Springholm's Goal-attack. How about that?'

Karen was utterly flabbergasted. Often enough she had made it known that it was her dearest wish to switch from defending to shooting. She thought that if ever Julie or Rebecca couldn't play then she herself was the natural replacement for either of them. It was beyond her belief that anyone as chubby and ordinary as Keeley could be chosen for the position she coveted.

She was about to rush off to complain to Rebecca and Julie when she saw that they had left the court. Instead, she expressed her feelings pretty forcibly to Zoe, who listened and nodded and listened and nodded. Zoe hardly ever disagreed with Karen about anything.

Zoe thought life was tough enough without adding to it the extra burden of any dispute with the voluble Karen. Keeley wasn't troubled by their reaction. She had enough self-awareness to know that everyone else in the Springholm squad would be surprised at her selection for the Cup tie. But nothing was now going to reduce her enjoyment of the occasion.

The arrival of the Netherlee team halted discussion of what Karen and Tara Morton were describing as an eccentric decision by Rebecca. Tara, who played Centre, was also dismayed by Keeley's selection because she felt her own place was threatened; if Keeley played really well then she might be retained in the team when Julie resumed her role. And in that event Keeley would probably be switched to Centre to displace Tara! Tara shuddered at that thought. Her best move, therefore, was to play so outstandingly against Netherlee that she would secure the Centre position for herself for many matches to come. She studied the opposition with increased interest.

Netherlee looked as quiet as an outing of nuns. They were also, Tara decided, boring. Even their outfit was as dull as could be. French navy was the colour of their skirts, white for their blouses. Tara possessed an excellent memory. So far as she could tell this wasn't the same team they'd played in the League at the end of last season and utterly annihilated. Only one of the faces seemed familiar: a golden-haired, freckled girl with wide-apart eyes. Suddenly, Tara remembered her name: Andrea Shepherd. But, surely . . .

'I thought you played for Kenningham, Andrea,' she said, almost accusingly.

'Oh, I did, you're right. What a marvellous memory! But I've switched now. I get on a lot better with Netherlee.'

Andrea was smiling broadly. Tara recalled that she was very speedy indeed, a Wing-attack who played with verve and invention. Unless she'd lost her form completely there couldn't be any doubt she was the sort of player capable of revitalising a team. She wondered whether Rebecca knew that Netherlee had acquired such a dynamic new player.

'What do you think your chances are against us?' Tara inquired.

34

'Don't really know,' was the candid reply. 'But I do know we'll be trying as hard as we can. There's plenty of spirit as well as new faces in our team these days. I think if we find a bit of form we'll give you a good game.'

Somehow, as Netherlee players began to throw the ball about as a warming-up exercise, they looked to Tara to be a little less boring than she'd supposed at first. Julie, though, wasn't impressed when Tara gave her the news of Netherlee's new player.

'It always takes time for a newcomer to slot into any team,' she said fairly dismissively. Clearly it hadn't occurred to her that Keeley fitted into that category with Springholm. 'On top of that, I can't see one player making all that difference to a team like Netherlee. They needed a wholesale transfusion of new blood from what I remember of them.'

'If you say so...' murmured Tara, far from convinced.

Before the players took their places on the court Rebecca, as usual, had a few words to say to her team. She didn't particularly enjoy the task of trying to motivate the players; to her mind, no player should need to be told what was required of her and the rest of the team. It should be instinctive to go out there and play as well as possible.

Tactics, she supposed, were important; but she

would never allow herself or her team-mates to be ruled by tactical considerations. Netball was essentially a simple game: as long as players could catch and throw, run and jump, there couldn't be much wrong with them. All the girls in her team were intelligent enough to see for themselves what was needed from them. Nonetheless, she went through the routine of giving them a target and telling them not to be discouraged by any sudden and unexpected setback.

It was as well that she did.

For the time of year it was a fairly humid evening. Netherlee, however, began as if they were frozen and determined to get warm by ceaseless running and jumping. With almost bewildering speed, the ball went from hand to hand. Not a pass was dropped, not an interception was made by any of the Springholm players. Almost before she knew the game was in progress, Karen Honley conceded the first goal. Or that was how she felt when the ball went through the net for Netherlee's opening score. Her opponent was of fairly slight build; to many, she didn't look to have either the height or the strength to play Goal-shooter. But she could jump triumphantly and her aim when she had the ring in her sights was deadly. Karen should have been more alert to all that for those were the

identical attributes possessed by Julie France, their own Goal-attack. But, unwittingly, Karen relaxed when challenged, failed to cut off either the pass or route to goal, and so had the mortification of seeing Netherlee take the lead within a few seconds (or so it seemed) of the start of the Cup-tie.

Rebecca, viewing events from the other end of the court, swallowed hard. It was just as hard for her to believe that their opponents, that 'pathetic little outfit', as Julie had so pitilessly described them, were ahead. And ahead through some incisive, skilful play. There was nothing lucky about the way Netherlee had scored their goal. It was well worked and splendidly taken.

'Come on, Springholm, get a grip!' Rebecca muttered.

But it was said more to whip herself into action than to encourage, audibly, the rest of her players. She daren't look across the touchline to see what Julie's reaction was to this dreadful setback.

If Netherlee were jubilant they didn't allow it to show or to distract them from the task of adding to their score: and adding to it as swiftly as possible. They gave the appearance of being fit, disciplined and well trained. In Andrea Shepherd they also possessed a fine athlete and skipper, who plainly believed in leading by example.

After Tara had carelessly dropped the ball from a neat back pass by Rebecca, it was Andrea who seized possession and, cleverly changing the point of attack, exchanged passes with her Goal-attack. All the time she was angling for an opening but it came in an unexpected way. By swinging the ball from one direction to another she completely flummoxed Zoe Ablett, Springholm's Goal-defence. Next instant, Andrea had transferred the ball into the shooting circle for her Goal-shooter to take the pass, swing through almost 360 degrees, move back a pace and then shoot for goal. She was robbed of a score by the narrowest margin. The ball struck the rim as it came down, bounced up and then spun away behind the post.

'Whew!' Julie exclaimed.

She had seen at once what a threat Andrea Shepherd represented. It was obvious that the girl with the mane of gold-coloured hair was in prime form, and was undeniably talented. Unlike Tara, Julie didn't have a good memory for faces and the details of past events so she didn't remember where she'd seen Andrea before. This newcomer, however, had not only lifted their morale: she was drawing out the skills from other players that they'd kept hidden or hadn't known they possessed. The way she was playing, Andrea was a distinct threat to Springholm's hopes of reaching the next round of the Manor House Cup, the early season trophy that was coveted by every team in the League.

Julie was anxious to catch Rebecca's eye. She wanted to suggest a tactic that would suppress the threat from Andrea. If Netherlee's Wing-attack wasn't put under close marking then she would go on creating havoc in Springholm's ranks. Rebecca wasn't really aware of the extent of the threat yet. Her concern was with the fumbling among her own players. So far nobody had managed to set up a single positive move. Twice already Tara had been pulled up by the umpire for contact offences. It was plain that Tara was displaying great keenness, that she wanted to initiate attacks. But by being penalised in that way she was giving advantages to Netherlee. Zoe, too, was an offender, though in her case the errors were to do with obstruction. Nobody seemed capable of giving or receiving a clean, fast pass. For one reason or another, Springholm were about as sharp as a bowl of porridge.

So far Keeley hadn't touched the ball for more than a second or two. With Netherlee gaining, and usually keeping, possession, Springholm's attack hadn't been given an opportunity to function at all. Keeley, expecting to build up a profitable partnership with Rebecca, was beginning to despair.

She sensed that if Springholm didn't win this match convincingly then she'd *never* be given another chance to play Goal-attack. Her ambition would be buried before it had even been launched.

When, in rapid succession, Netherlee scored two more goals without reply all the Springholm players knew that their team was in a crisis.

Four

During a very brief stoppage, when a player was being cautioned, Julie at last managed to attract Rebecca's attention. Rebecca looked thoroughly puzzled as Julie gesticulated and tried to point out how to deal with the menace of Andrea Shepherd. Her idea now was that Carolyn Peachey, Springholm's Wing-attack, should stay in the centre third as much as possible to shadow Andrea and attempt to cut out the passes she was taking; and that Tara should mark Andrea when the Netherlee attacker was making a forward run.

The message, however, wasn't getting across (or, as Julie saw it, Rebecca was being a bit dim for once). Julie was on the point of explaining verbally when the umpire spotted her.

'I don't allow coaching or instructions being sent from off the court,' she said sternly. 'You should know that.'

'I wasn't doing that,' Julie lied as convincingly as she could. 'I was letting our captain know that one of our players is injured. Our Goal-attack, actually.'

The umpire, taken aback that her rebuke hadn't silenced the offender instantly, glanced at Keeley.

'She looks perfectly all right to me,' was her reaction.

'Oh, but she's a real heroine, she wouldn't let on that she was in pain,' Julie said with admiration in her voice.

The umpire wasn't the sort of woman who was ever willing to lose an argument, especially when she was in a role of authority. She frowned at Julie and said: 'I'll decide whether she's fit or not.'

That exchange, however, had been audible to Rebecca, now looking, if possible, still more baffled by Julie's attitude. As soon as the umpire's back was turned Julie mouthed as distinctly as possible while pointing directly at Keeley: 'Get her OFF!'

Her timing, though, could hardly have been worse. The very next moment Carrie Peachey brought off a quite brilliant interception by anticipating Andrea's low pass; then, after a swift exchange with Tara, she flung the ball hard to Rebecca. One of Rebecca's neatest tricks was a jinking sidestep and this time she employed it to good effect to outwit her marker as she took the ball almost at full stretch.

Keeley had intelligently moved into, and then out of, the shooting circle in an effort to elude her own marker, Netherlee's towering Goal-defence. For once, Keeley's bulk was to her advantage. Her opponent simply couldn't get round her as Keeley swung first one way, then another, shielding the ball she'd just received from Rebecca until she could aim for goal. A more experienced shooter would have stepped back a pace before letting the ball go – but she still almost scored. The ball ricocheted from the rim and Rebecca, timing her jump perfectly, reached it ahead of her opponents. Effortlessly, she lobbed it through the ring for Springholm's first goal.

Keeley's joy in what had been achieved was enormous. She couldn't have been happier if she'd scored herself. Rebecca, inevitably, had signalled her congratulations as they all moved back to the centre. She had done it in just the way she did when Julie was her team-mate. That was not lost on Keeley.

Of course, by itself one goal hardly mattered at all. Netherlee were well ahead. But that goal demonstrated that Springholm could fight back – and were fighting back.

Carrie Peachey, for one, now felt that her worst moments were over: she had re-discovered her usual

45

form. A slim, short-haired girl with an outwardly sunny disposition, she worried more about her game than anyone would ever have believed. She knew she wasn't, by some distance, the best player in the team and she feared that one day Julie and Rebecca would find a replacement for her. So she wanted to impress with everything she did, without making her intention obvious. Now she was fully aware that Julie must have taken note of her contribution to that goal. Carrie had the idea that Julie didn't care for her at all, either as a person or as a netball player. When Julie addressed her as 'Peaches' she felt it was always in a mocking fashion.

Julie was thinking only about Keeley and how she could remove her from the game. One near-success at shooting didn't, in Julie's view, compensate for Keeley's overall lack of skill as an attacking player. With Springholm now trailing by three goals to one to a team that should have been swept out of the competition by the end of the first quarter something drastic had to be done. Tara was not having a particularly good game and it occurred to Julie that the best change might be for Keeley to switch with Tara at half-time while she herself resumed her shooting role.

Rebecca, however, didn't see it like that at the first interval when Julie explained her ideas.

'I think Keeley's doing pretty well considering her lack of experience,' the captain told her friend. 'I couldn't take her off now. It would ruin her confidence for, oh, goodness knows how long. I agree that Tara isn't playing well but –'

'Look, Becky, if we don't make changes quickly we'll lose this tie. Nothing more certain. And if we lose this tie and have nothing to aim for then I'll find somebody else to play for. I'm not turning out for a team of losers.'

Rebecca stared at her in disbelief. 'You're joking, Julie. You couldn't –'

'Rebecca, you know me. I don't joke about sport. It's too serious for that – well, it is to me. You know I always play to win. So I'm not playing for losers.'

'But you're the one who insisted Netherlee were rubbish, that we could beat them with one hand tied behind our backs.'

'O.K., so I was wrong about that. I admit it. But this isn't the team we thrashed last season. They're on the up-and-up. That golden girl at Wing-attack has given 'em new life. I told you, she's got to be stopped. Well, Keeley could just about manage that, I reckon. She could flatten her if she needed to, put her out of the game. But she can't do it if she stays in my position. You know that.'

She paused and then hurried on: 'So, come on,

Becky, it's shift *la* Hilton or lose me. I know we're mates but you're captain and you've got to decide. I've told you what I think. And I'm not usually wrong about netball in spite of my mistake about Netherlee.'

It was one of Rebecca's strengths that she could recognise when someone else's point of view made more sense than her own. Her friendship with Julie was based on candour as well as kindness. So she was always able to react decisively when necessary even if her own instinct might be to pursue a policy of wait and see.

'O.K.,' she said, 'I'll do it. You come on at half-time and take Keeley's place. She can go in the Centre spot. I don't think it'll do much for her ego but that can't be helped. You're right, Julie: we've got to get a grip on this game. We've got to rattle Netherlee out of their composure.'

Julie had to be content with that even though she felt that time was being wasted and opportunities thrown away because changes weren't taking place immediately.

Yet it was Springholm who scored next following a good move between Tara and Carolyn which led to Rebecca putting the ball in the net from the very perimeter of the shooting circle. One of the things that Rebecca and Julie had in common was that nothing seemed to disturb their concentration when they had a chance of scoring.

That effort, though, was almost at once cancelled out by another score by Netherlee. For no apparent reason Zoe Ablett simply dropped the ball instead of throwing it. Andrea, her nearest opponent, didn't miss openings like that. Before Zoe could even open her mouth to apologise (it was in her nature to apologise for any mishap in which she was involved) Andrea had seized the ball and whipped it across to her Goal-shooter. Karen, who was on the point of reprimanding Zoe for her error, took her eye off her opponent ... and suffered the consequence. The Netherlee shooter scored with some ease.

Julie ground her teeth and tugged angrily at the scarlet band which kept her fair hair in place. Never had she more regretted not being on court. Although Rebecca was captain (and deserved to be, in her friend's opinion), Julie always took a leading role in running the team; and the rest of the players respected her tactical views as well as her playing skills. They would accept her advice. So Julie wouldn't have hesitated to have a few words with Zoe about sharpening up. In fact, as Rebecca could have warned her, that sort of approach wouldn't work with Zoe. She had to be praised, not punished with words. Karen was one who reacted best to severe criticism and the comment that she was letting herself down as much as the team when she committed mistakes.

'Come on Springholm, you're not *trying*!' Julie yelled, much to the surprise of most of her team-mates. No one had ever accused them of lack of effort before in public. Zoe, inevitably, assumed she was the real target. Her inclination thereafter was to avoid the ball as much as possible. So her play declined still further, to Julie's disgust. She had long felt that Springholm needed a more competent Goal-defence.

Karen, however, had quickly learned her lesson after Netherlee's fifth goal. From then on she began to play with mounting assurance. She even ventured out more often into the defence third, not only to check Netherlee's attacks but to initiate attacking play by her own side. From that point on Springholm gradually began to display more evidence of real teamwork.

As half-time approached it was obvious that several of the players were feeling the effects of the airless, sticky evening. Infringements increased and the umpire seemed to be on the point of losing her temper at one stage. Her reprimand to Netherlee's Centre for a really quite minor stepping offence was unnecessarily fierce. The girl showed her resent-

ment through a fascinating range of facial contortions when the umpire wasn't looking. Moments later there was another clash between the same girl and Keeley. This was a collision between two players eager to gain possession when the ball was dropped. But Keeley was off-balance when they bumped into each other and went sprawling; she grazed a knee and an elbow and was shaken but not seriously hurt. Her injuries won the sympathy of the umpire who gave the Netherlee player a very stern warning about her conduct.

'One more trick like that, young lady, and you will be taking no further part in this match,' were the actual words used.

While that was being said Keeley dabbed with a handkerchief at her grazes and looked close to tears. She didn't say anything to support the Netherlee Centre who insisted to the umpire that the collision was a pure accident. Keeley didn't think it was an accident and she was fed up with being victimised. Her intuition told her that the match was beginning to go wrong for her. She sensed that Julie was just waiting for the right moment to come on in her place. The one person free at the moment to help an injured team-mate was Julie: and Julie stayed where she was, on the touchline, apparently indifferent to Keeley's misfortune.

'Are you all right, Kee?' inquired Rebecca, coming across to assess the extent of the injury.

'Well, it does hurt a lot,' Keeley admitted. 'But I expect –'

'You can go off for a rest, if you like,' Rebecca offered swiftly. 'I mean, we can substitute you easily enough. Now we're losing we can't afford to carry an injured player.'

Rebecca felt she couldn't tell Keeley it was better to go off now than be replaced at half-time. That's what she wanted to do but Keeley's feelings had to be taken into consideration. It was something that mattered much less to Julie who was always prepared to sacrifice the individual for the good of the cause.

'I'll – I'll see how it feels when I'm moving about,' Keeley suggested. 'I'll tell you if it's really bad.'

'O.K., but don't hold back. We've got to win this match. So everybody has to give one hundred per cent.'

Netherlee's Centre wasn't holding back. Having noted that Keeley didn't retaliate after their far from accidental collision she took an early opportunity to emphasise her physical superiority over the red haired Springholm player. The next time Keeley was in close proximity to her the Centre, making sure she was unobserved by the umpire, backed into her and viciously drove her heel into Keeley's ankle. Keeley gasped with pain and might have hit back but for the fact that the agile Centre had already danced out of range. Julie, who hadn't seen the kick but heard Keeley's anguished cry, assumed it was the original injury that was troubling her.

When half-time came Julie was on the court in an instant.

'Come on,' she said urgently to Keeley, 'I need your – my – bib. I'm back in action for the second half.'

Keeley looked stunned, even though she'd guessed what would happen. She shot an appealing look at Rebecca. If Rebecca thought she should continue playing, she would continue.

'Yes, I think you should change places with Julie,' Rebecca agreed softly. 'I don't want you to aggravate your injuries, Kee. We're going to need you for another match.'

Rebecca had been considering Julie's other proposal that Keeley should take Tara's place as Centre; but she'd decided against it. Keeley was not only damaged; she looked defeated.

'Hard luck, Keeley,' said Carolyn Peachey with unexpected sympathy. 'I saw what their Centre did – when she kicked you, I mean. You know, you should have clouted her back. She deserves it. She's the sort who'll always go on niggling at you if you don't hit back and show you're as tough as her.'

'There you are, Keeley, that's good advice,' said Julie, with a laugh. 'Stand up for yourself. Hit back!'

Keeley, surprised by this support, didn't know how to answer. But she was grateful for Carolyn's attitude.

'I would hit her if I had some boxing gloves,' she said as a joke. 'I just wouldn't want to soil my bare hands on her.'

'Well, my brother's got some old boxing gloves he doesn't use any more so you can have those if you like,' said Carolyn, taking the remark seriously.

Rebecca, sensing something about Keeley but not knowing what it was, glanced across at her. She could see that Keeley was struggling to reach some sort of decision. It was a moment to give her team-mate further support.

'Yes, I reckon that's good advice, Kee. Stick up for yourself, otherwise you'll always be trodden under. Nothing the bully likes better than the victim who just soaks up all the punishment. Now, let's get to grips with this game again; we're still in trouble and we've got to find a way out of it. Tara, I want you to be a bit more positive from now on. You're hesitating before throwing the ball. It's as if you didn't know who to throw it *to*. We need a much faster service. O.K.?'

'O.K.,' agreed Tara, keeping to herself the thought that it was a bit unfair to pick on her for criticism. In her view, she hadn't played badly: indeed, she'd been in better form than Zoe and Karen.

Rebecca's advice to Zoe was tempered by the warmth of the smile that accompanied it. She didn't want to see Zoe dissolve into tears. The captain had enough problems to deal with without having to comfort the temperamental.

'I could change places with someone, if you like,' Karen volunteered. 'I mean, it's a warm night and I haven't been rushing around like some people. Maybe I have spare energy.'

'Nice one, *la* Honley, but you're a keeper, not a shooter, and we're not short of shooters,' Julie remarked.

Rebecca shook her head at that. It was a tactless rejection of Karen's offer and Julie wasn't even being asked to surrender her role. But when she was in the mood to hand out advice Julie was difficult to suppress.

'No, we'll keep our standard formation and make the most of our experience,' Rebecca said soothingly. 'If you can keep Netherlee's shooters quiet, Karen, you'll be doing the best possible job for us. So, come on, girls, we've got to go all out for this win. We must put them under pressure *instantly*.'

In fact, Netherlee must have felt they were being hit by a whirlwind when the match resumed. Tara feinted to throw to a defender and then cleverly supplied a pass to Carolyn who, in turn, dummied to send the ball to Rebecca and actually gave it to Julie. Few players were faster around the court than Julie and the quickness of her movements as she exchanged with Rebecca and then Tara were

56

bewildering for players and spectators alike. A brilliant exchange of passes on the boundary of the shooting circle presented Rebecca with a scoring chance which she took with rare nonchalance.

So, within seconds of the start of the second half, Springholm had cut the deficit to two goals. More importantly, that score was secured in such a way that confidence immediately began to flow back into the Springholm ranks. The other players were aware that the striking partnership between their two shooters had re-formed as if it had never been broken. The instinctive passing, the anticipation of each other's positional moves, the confidence in their shooting: these qualities had been demonstrated in scintillating fashion.

Keeley watched silently. She knew she ought to be cheering the goal that put Springholm back in the game; she ought to be thrilled for Julie's sake that the goal had been created by her speed and enterprise. But for the moment Keeley couldn't bring herself to celebrate. After all, her own play in that position, Goal-attack, was now seen to be ineffectual. She couldn't be compared with Julie. She couldn't be regarded as a true substitute. In her own play she hadn't revealed any of the assets Julie possessed and had just called on.

A few moments later Keeley turned away and

limped towards the changing-rooms. She wasn't turning her back on the game simply because she was no longer in the line-up. Her grazes, and the ankle that had been kicked, were still paining her. A hot shower was what she needed and was going to have. At least she'd have the showers to herself and she would enjoy that. She wouldn't suffer the pangs of envy that sometimes assailed her when she noted how slim and elegant some of the other girls were. She wished she had a figure like Rebecca and Julie, Karen and Carrie. Even before she reached the changing-room she was thinking that Carolyn's idea of putting on boxing gloves to use in an emergency was interesting. It wasn't as far-fetched as some people might think. There was just a possibility it could help to solve one of her problems. She'd give it serious thought.

None of the other players was aware of Keeley's departure. Now that the scores were almost level the match had become absorbing. Netherlee, anxious to pull off a shock victory that would boost their morale as nothing else could, weren't going to concede anything. Andrea Shepherd had also delivered a pep talk at the interval and her team-mates desperately wanted to follow her instructions. But Springholm held the initiative after scoring so early in the second half: and they weren't going to surrender it.

Julie was again the mainspring of the next attack and the ball was hurled from one side of the court to the other and back again in a clever attempt to disguise the direction from which the threat would come. Carrie now appeared to be in sparkling form as she more than once combined with Julie to set up an opening. Julie pulled off one of her most adroit tricks by switching the ball from one hand to the other behind her back and then firing it hard at Rebecca. It was a manoeuvre she and Rebecca had rehearsed umpteen times and so Rebecca knew what was coming. As she sprang to catch the ball she was already lining up her shot. The split-second she touched down she sent the ball on its way through the goal.

It was that goal that really killed off Netherlee's hopes if not their spirit. Another goal, a minute later, from Julie on the very edge of the shooting circle, just when everyone was expecting her to pass, brought the scores level. But by then Andrea had begun to sense that the tie was slipping from Netherlee's grasp. The partnership between the opposition's shooters was devastating. It was even better than the last time Andrea had seen Julie and Rebecca in action. It was, she reflected sadly, a great pity that the podgy red-haired girl had been injured and replaced. Had she stayed on court then Netherlee would surely have held on to their lead. Andrea couldn't help wishing that she had joined Springholm instead of Netherlee.

She did her best to rally her side but although they did manage another goal two minutes from the end it wasn't enough. By then Springholm were leading by four goals and the outcome of the Cup-tie was in no doubt at all. The Shooters were as good as in the next round already.

It was Rebecca who recorded Springholm's final goal, one that really only she could have managed. Once again Carrie was the instigator, feinting to go one way, then another before collecting the ball from Tara and then sending it looping high into the shooting circle. Springholm's skipper rose almost lazily to meet the pass: but because of her timing she seemed half-a-metre higher than Netherlee's Goalkeeper when she took the ball and flicked it sideways through the ring.

'You see, it was easy after all,' Julie exulted when the umpire signalled the end of the match. 'I told you we'd trounce them once we took *la* Hilton off.'

Courteously, Rebecca shook hands with each of their opponents and then commiserated with Andrea Shepherd. It had been a very close thing and she knew Julie realised that; the final score undoubtedly flattered Springholm. But to Julie the result was all that mattered. She wouldn't even think about Springholm's problems until the team assembled for the next match. She wouldn't concern herself with the worries that must be afflicting some of her team-mates. Julie, as she sometimes laughingly remarked, just took each match as it came along.

Rebecca, however, was conscious of several problems that would have to be sorted out without delay if Springholm were to have any hope of making real progress in their quest for the Manor House Cup. And not all of those problems concerned playing skills and tactics.

Five

Two days later Keeley Hilton was walking home from school when she encountered Sandra Renshaw with another girl and two older boys. Keeley recognised one of them as Linton McCloud, tall, blond-haired and unquestionably attractive. He was the one Sandra had set her heart on: she'd once confided to Keeley when they were still best friends. His name alone, she breathlessly added, was 'fabulous, just fabulous'. In those days Linton wouldn't even look in Sandra's direction: his passion was for a rather plain, bespectacled, frowning girl called Lizzie. Sandra had wanted to terrorise Lizzie out of Linton's life. Now, it seemed, she was getting her way for she and Linton had their arms, and almost their entire bodies, entwined as they gossiped beside the entrance to a narrow alleyway that led to the bus station. If she was to catch her usual bus then Keeley had to use that alleyway.

'Well, look who it is, the fat girl who lets a teeny-weeny, hardly-visible scratch keep her off games,' jeered Sandra. ' "Can't play hockey, miss, 'cos I've bumped my fat little, precious little arm. Sorry, miss, it really hurts, miss".'

The other three bystanders dutifully laughed. Sandra had always been a leader.

'Such a *huge* scratch – look at it,' continued Sandra.

And to everyone's surprise she suddenly disentangled herself from Linton and grabbed at Keeley's elbow. By sheer misfortune, she grasped Keeley on the rawest part of her wound, a deep graze that ran almost the length of her forearm.

Keeley couldn't help yelling with the pain. Instinctively, she swung her free arm at Sandra and her fist struck her former friend on the chest. Surprised by this unprecedented reaction to her customary taunting, Sandra staggered back, marginally off-balance.

'Hey, you leave my girl alone!' yelled Linton, jumping forward to restrain Keeley. He never needed an excuse to put his hands on a girl, especially one as pretty as Keeley.

Keeley outwitted them all by the way she ducked out of range – and astonished them with the speed she displayed as she shot down the alleyway. Her training for netball was paying off for once. To her relief they didn't pursue her. Instead they resumed their clinch, with Linton making exaggerated pleas to his girl friend to be allowed to examine any injuries she might have suffered in Keeley's dreadful assault on her. Sandra just giggled and said later would do just as well.

Keeley didn't slow down until she'd reached the end of the alleyway. Somehow she managed to feel both deflated and elated at the same time; deflated because she'd run away from such a minor incident, elated because, at last, she'd hit back at Sandra. Really hit back. Instead of cowering under Sandra's spite and insults, she'd retaliated and that did much for her self-esteem. As she waited for her bus she wondered whether Sandra would now stop her campaign against her. If not, then she ought to be ready to deal with her again: and deal with her in such a way that Sandra would never resume her rotten conduct. She remembered the offer Carolyn Peachey had made during the netball match to lend her some boxing gloves. The more Keeley thought about it the more sensible it was.

Carolyn lived not far from Keeley's home so it was no effort to make a digression when she got off the bus. By now the pain in her elbow had more or less subsided, though Keeley caressed the long graze as she walked along. It was the deliberate kick on the ankle from Netherlee's Centre that hurt the worst. She hadn't expected another netball player to behave so maliciously. Still, she could imagine Julie reacting in much the same way if she wanted to get back at an opponent. Julie would stop at nothing to achieve success.

Keeley knew that she had no real hope of taking Julie's place in attack ever again. But she prayed that her performance in partnership with Rebecca was creditable enough for her to be given another chance in the team. She didn't mind where they played her just so long as she was in the team. After the Netherlee game she desperately wanted to have a chat with Rebecca; but Rebecca simply wasn't easy to talk to after a match. Once it was over she seemed to switch off. Still, she wasn't much more approachable at other times. Rebecca often had an air of aloofness. Keeley found it almost impossible to open a conversation with her when she was in that distant, detached mood. Yet that in no way diminished the admiration she felt for Rebecca, her natural skills, her instinctive leadership and, of course, her marvellously slender figure.

Carrie, thankfully, was in when Keeley rang the front doorbell; and she seemed not at all surprised that her team-mate wanted to take up the offer of a loan of a pair of boxing gloves.

'I think you're doing absolutely the right thing in learning to defend yourself, Kee,' she declared as she led the way to her bedroom.

'Honestly, some people these days just think they can get away with murder. If you don't try to stop 'em you're the dead one, sooner or later. I'm not very big as you can see but I don't believe in letting anyone jump on me. I'll go for them if I have to. Jon – he's my brother – is just the same. Same sort of build, too. That's why he got the gloves. And they've worked for him. No one tries twice to knock Jon about! I was so impressed with what he could do that I had a go myself. A pair of boxing gloves can give you a real feeling of confidence, Keeley – yes, even if you're not wearing 'em. Once you've had a good work-out with gloves you know how to handle yourself, if you see what I mean. You'll just feel good.'

Keeley did see. Carrie had expressed exactly what was in her own mind. Although they'd been members of the same netball squad for almost a year she'd never taken much notice of the petite girl, who usually played at Wing-attack. Carrie managed to be both cheerful and serious at the same time and Keeley felt perhaps she'd ignored her because she didn't know her real personality.

'I didn't know you went in for gymnastics, you never told us,' Keeley remarked as she glanced at the colour photographs in leather frames on top of a chest of drawers.

'I don't tell everyone everything, you know,' Carolyn replied airily, though she grinned as she said it. 'I also like flower arranging but nobody's interested in that, except other flower arrangers, of course.'

It was a large room and brightly decorated in orange and green. Keeley, thinking of her own enlarged cupboard, as she described it, experienced another pang of envy.

'I expect gymnastics is useful training for netball,' she said as Carolyn dragged a large suitcase from under her bed and opened it to reveal a jumble of sporting equipment.

'You could say that,' Carolyn agreed. 'Here, try these on for size.'

The gloves were altogether bulkier than Keeley had supposed and they felt terribly cumbersome as she pulled them on with Carolyn's necessary assistance. On the other hand, they looked both dangerous and impressive. Keeley automatically hunched her shoulders and adopted a belligerent posture, imitating the boxers she'd seen on TV.

'Very good,' Carolyn approved. 'To keep them on

in a real fight they have to be taped to your wrists but I don't think we'll bother with that today. You'll be able to get in some punching practice without risk of them slipping off all the time. Anyway, Kee, best of luck with them. Hope they give you what the experts are supposed to call the ring of confidence. *Boxing* ring. Get it?'

They laughed together and, a few minutes later, Keeley left. As she used a duffel bag for her school things she was able to conceal the gloves from prying eyes. Her family simply wouldn't understand what she was up to, especially as she'd never mentioned Sandra's hostility. Fortunately, there was no one else in when she got home. So she was able to go straight to the garage that belonged to the flat where she lived. It was one of a row of garages beside the parking area behind the tower block; her father would be at work for at least another hour and even then there was no guarantee he'd drive straight home. She had ample time for a good work-out.

At the back of the garage was an old mattress her grandmother had discarded and asked Keeley's father to dispose of for her. Of course, as usual, he'd done nothing after slinging it in a corner of the garage.

For Keeley's purpose, it was ideal. Using some other jumble to keep it in place she propped it upright. Then she wound some thick twine around a couple of the exposed springs (the bed had borne her grandmother's considerable weight for rather too many years before giving way in a number of places) and attached each end to hooks on the wooden door frame. It was a rather makeshift arrangement: and yet there was no doubt it did in a way resemble a sort of punch-bag.

With eager anticipation Keeley donned the gloves, did a bit of shadow boxing to warm up, and then rammed a left and a right into the sagging

mattress. To her delight, her hands didn't hurt at all: but she was sure the mattress was suffering.

She paused to do a little skipping and then waded into the enemy again, left-right-left, in rapid succession. When she began she hadn't thought of the mattress as representing any particular person: and she didn't want to feel that she was battering away at someone she knew. All the same, images of the grandmother who'd treated her worse than a servant and then of Sandra kept flitting across her mind. Whether these visions added extra force to her punching, she couldn't tell; she didn't want to know about any motive other than the vital one of defending herself.

Still, something seemed to be inspiring her as she hit hard, left, right, left, RIGHT! The work-out was proving to be exactly the tonic she needed at the end of a rotten day.

Six

Two hours later Carolyn Peachey received two more visitors; but this time they came by her invitation. That invitation was a complete surprise to Rebecca and Julie, who'd been walking through the town centre, deep in a discussion about pop concerts. Carrie, pleased by the warmth of their greeting, had on the spur of the moment invited them to come round to her house one evening to listen to her collection of records. What Carrie didn't know was that her play in the later stages of the Cup-tie with Netherlee had impressed both of them.

Julie, as usual, had previously been dismissive of Carrie's abilities: but she admitted to Rebecca that she'd changed her mind after noting Carrie's inventive and energetic performance as Springholm battled to get on level terms and then surged ahead. Rebecca, too, had had doubts about her. She feared that the slightly-built girl with the very short, dark

72

hair might lack stamina as well as commitment. Because Carolyn could switch from sunny to serious in no time at all Rebecca wondered whether she was plagued by worries about her game. But her view changed when she saw how enthusiastic and excited Carolyn was after the Netherlee match.

'Hey, what a zazzy room this is,' exclaimed Julie as she entered Carrie's bedroom.

'Zazzy' was a word Julie employed widely to describe anything at all that met with her total approval.

Carrie was amused by the way Julie wandered round the room in a very possessive manner, examining this and scrutinising that and nodding appreciatively over something else. She picked up a hairbrush and tried a couple of strokes on her own hair.

Rebecca, looking slightly disapproving of Julie's antics, sank on to the bed and leaned against the wall. She, too, liked the room, especially its spaciousness and modern furniture, but she thought Julie was supplying all the comments necessary. Julie, she reflected, really was a contradictory creature; only a few days ago she had said that Carolyn was a bit of a bore, someone who never had anything constructive to say about anything. Yet now she was chatting to Carrie in the most animated fashion about gymnastics and clothes, musical instruments (Julie occasionally played the drums whereas Carolyn was a more than able guitarist) and the range of posters that adorned three of the walls of the room, holidays on barges and the irritating habits of brothers, whether older or younger.

Then, as Julie at last subsided on the duvet, Carolyn broached the topic she'd been wanting to discuss with the other two girls. She still hadn't any idea at all how they would react to it. The past few minutes in Julie's company had almost convinced her that Julie, for one, would be against it.

'Talking of boys,' she remarked as casually as possible while settling down on her own bed so that all three of them were now in a row, 'I had a thought the other day. Something, really, sparked off by what my brother Jon was saying. I don't know if I told you but Jon's a basketball fanatic – among other things! And we were arguing about the merits of basketball against netball, you know, which was faster and more skilful and which players were the fittest. Jon, typical for a boy, claimed that any really ordinary basketball team could beat any really good netball side. I told him that was rubbish. Naturally!

'Jon replied it could easily be proved because his basketball team would play us at netball and could *guarantee* to win. I said, if I could persuade the other girls to give it a go, he was on – we'd prove we were the best at our own sport, however terrific the boys think they are at whatever they play. I mean, it wouldn't be bad training for us, would it, practising against bigger and stronger, physically stronger, players?'

She paused. The other two hadn't given a hint of what they were thinking. Neither had attempted to interrupt her.

'What – what do you think, then? Rebecca? Julie?'

'I'm – I'm not sure,' Rebecca replied, sounding as

hesitant as she felt. 'I think it may well be, well, risky. The boys will just be aggressive, I suppose. They'll want to show off.'

'I think it's a *great* idea!' Julie enthused. 'Terrific. Really zazzy. It'll really sharpen us up, give us a chance to see how to overcome bigger and tougher – oh, and *awkward* – opponents. They'll have to play by our rules, official netball rules, and so they'll be at a big disadvantage. I reckon we'll show 'em a thing or two and that'll be good for morale, *our* morale. Also, it'll be zazzy to put a few boys in their places.

'Peaches, you're a genius for thinking of it!'

So taken was she with the idea that she turned, ran her hand through Carolyn's hair and then swoopingly kissed her lightly on the cheek.

Carolyn, startled, managed to cover her surprise with a grin. She could never have predicted that Julie would be so approving.

'But, listen, if we lose to the boys – and there must be a big chance of that because of their brute strength if nothing else – if we lose to them it will be *bad* for our morale,' Rebecca pointed out. 'Our confidence, which has been a bit shaky lately anyway, will start to drain away. Disastrous that would be. No, I'd be very cautious about fixing up a game like that.'

'Oh, come on, Becky, let's be a bit more positive. It's not like you to be, well, so weak,' Julie told her. 'You know my views that weak opposition's no good for anybody. A team improves by playing teams as good or better than themselves. Well, a boys' team is bound to give us an opportunity to test ourselves against physically superior opponents. That could help to toughen up our weak links. Like Zoe. If she can defend against a boy it'll do her a power of good. Even if she can't she won't lose anything by that.

'And the feeble Keeley. She's *big* enough, so she could get a boost by proving she can compete with a boy. If, that is, she doesn't dissolve into a tear-drop at the very thought of facing a lad in competition! After all, even an ordinary girl player can put the terrors up *la* Hilton.'

'Actually, I think Keeley isn't as feeble as you imagine, Julie,' Carolyn told her. 'She wants to defend herself and she's perfectly willing to learn how to do it. In fact, she's just borrowed a pair of Jon's old boxing gloves to get in the right mood!'

Julie looked amazed. 'I'll believe it when I see it. Still, must be a step in the right direction.'

'I'm worried about Keeley,' Rebecca admitted. 'I think she's in some sort of trouble that she can't talk about. I tried to, well, hint that we'd help if we could but she sheered away from the subject.'

77

'Well, if she got somebody to teach her boxing, or just learns how to use those gloves, she should be able to sort things out,' Julie replied cheerfully. 'Do her a power of good if she can cope on her own.'

Rebecca doubted if things were ever sorted out as easily as that but she didn't want to go on about Keeley's problems. She was well aware that the others didn't view the red-haired girl in the same light; but then, they weren't captaining Springholm and so didn't have to worry about other players.

'Going back to the suggestion of a training session with boys,' Rebecca resumed, 'can I inquire where you think we should hold it, Carrie? I can see problems if we simply try to arrange it at a leisure centre.'

Carrie shrugged. 'Don't know. But I'm sure we'll be able to fix up something that suits everybody.'

'And *when* is it going to be?' Rebecca wanted to know next. 'We can't afford to have it too close to one of our League games or Cup fixtures in case we suffer any injuries. And there's bound to be a risk of that.'

'Look,' said Julie forcefully, 'there's risk in everything in life, Becky. Of *course* we may have a bit of a physical problem with the opposition. But I've already told you, that'll be for the good in the long run. There are benefits from testing ourselves

78

against different opposition, and this team will be different, all right. If it doesn't work out, so what? At least we'll have tried to improve ourselves. That's what counts.'

'I agree,' Carrie murmured.

'There you are then, Becky, you're outnumbered!' Julie declared but she was careful not to make it sound like a triumph. She hadn't lost her sense of loyalty to her erstwhile best friend.

'I didn't know we were voting,' said Rebecca coolly. 'I didn't know that Carolyn was one of the selectors, one of the committee.'

'We don't *have* a committee and you know that, Becky,' was the spirited response. 'Anyway, it was her idea in the first place and so she's entitled to have her say and vote.'

Rebecca knew there was no point in arguing and so gracefully she conceded the point. If the other two were so keen to hold the practice match against the boys then she wouldn't raise any further objections. Unanimity of outlook was something she was forever striving to achieve for the Shooters.

'Well,' said Rebecca, getting to her feet, 'I'll leave it to you two to fix the details, bearing in mind our fixture list and the availability of all the players. If you need my help or whatever, just let me know.'

At that moment she had no idea whether Julie

79

would leave with her or find an excuse (though one was hardly needed) to stay with Carolyn. Julie herself seemed uncertain what to do. Then, after a brief hesitation, she gave Carrie a quick hug and stood up.

'Great!' she exclaimed with enthusiasm that suddenly sounded rather artificial. 'We'll get things fixed up and then show the boys a thing or two! Then, well, if we win, that'll be really zazzy. O.K., Carrie, I'll be in touch. See you.'

Carolyn gave her a warm smile. 'Good. See you.'

Seven

The boys hadn't arrived when the Springholm players turned up at Logan Hall early one evening a few weeks later. That immediately led to speculation by some members of the squad, and Karen Honley in particular, that the basketball players had decided not to go ahead with the challenge match.

'Stands to reason,' Karen pointed out. 'They just won't want to lose face, and they certainly will lose face with their mates when we beat 'em! They'll have chickened out, you can bet on it. Disappointing, though.'

Tara laughed. 'You're not disappointed about the *match*, Karen. You're disappointed because you reckoned one of the boys would really fancy you. All boys are supposed to go for blondes with long hair, aren't they?'

'We can't all be winners,' Karen replied, ending that unprofitable line of comment.

'They'll turn up, all right,' Carolyn insisted. 'That's the way they'd lose face, by having it spread around that they hadn't the guts to play a girls' team at netball. I know most of my brother's mates and I'd make sure they all heard about the Bouncers' failure.'

'Dead right,' Julie agreed. 'We'd *all* spread the word.'

Brockwood Bouncers' basketball team had actually seemed very enthusiastic about the idea of the match, according to Jon Peachey. They had seen it not so much as a challenge as an opportunity to vary what they described as their rather boring training routine. They hadn't a doubt in their heads they would win. The fact they were playing netball, not basketball, made no difference at all, they claimed.

Naturally Carolyn and Julie pointed out that they wouldn't be able to live up to their name by bouncing the ball so much; they'd have to observe netball rules to the letter and accept that penalties would be awarded against them for stepping offences. Rebecca, when Carrie and Julie confirmed that the match was definitely on, had decided that it might be best if she acted as umpire. Brockwood had been invited to supply a second umpire but replied that they were perfectly happy to have the Shooters' skipper in sole charge.

Rebecca still wasn't sure they were doing the right thing. She didn't want her team-mates to suppose she was shirking the physical challenge of the contest; equally she didn't want to be bounced around by opponents (of course, there had been no end of jokes about Brockwood's name). It also seemed best for her to be in a position to insist on fair play and to crack down on offenders. However, she had let it be known that she reserved the right to join in the match in later stages if she wished. A team-mate would take over as umpire if Brockwood didn't care to supply a replacement for that role.

'Looking forward to the match?' she asked Keeley, who was to play as Goal-attack with Julie as Goal-shooter.

'Oh sure,' Keeley said, smiling quite broadly. 'I mean, these boys can't be worse than some of the girls when it comes to the rough stuff, can they?'

It wasn't really a question but Rebecca answered all the same. 'Don't be too sure,' she said cautiously.

Then, before anyone could exchange another word, the Bouncers arrived.

'Oh Lord,' murmured Zoe Ablett, 'they're even bigger than I thought they'd be.'

'And beefier!' Tara agreed.

Keeley, who'd been going through her now daily routine of squat thrusts and knees-up jumping on the spot, saw at once that Linton McCloud was in the party. In the same instant he caught sight of her: and grinned. What he said to one of his mates Keeley couldn't hear but she could make a guess. It had never occurred to her that Sandra's boyfriend, if that's what he still was, would be a member of the basketball team; but, naturally, his height would give him at least one advantage at that game. She would have to avoid any direct confrontation with him.

Quickly she glanced round the hall to see whether the Bouncers had brought any supporters with them; and, if so, whether Sandra was among them. Keeley knew she wouldn't be able to play at all if Sandra were on the sidelines, disparaging her play and urging her boyfriend on to greater efforts. Thankfully, however, there was no sign of Sandra. It appeared that the Bouncers had come alone, perhaps because they didn't want their friends to know they were playing girls at netball.

Jon Peachey, who seemed almost as slim as his sister, was to captain the Bouncers in honour of the occasion, though, as Carrie pointed out to her team-mates, he'd never skippered them at basketball. Although the boys firmly declined to wear the usual netball bibs they'd promised to abide by the rules that governed each player's territorial movements. Rebecca wasn't pleased. The absence of positional identification was going to make her job much harder. But, as Jon told her with the wide smile that was obviously a family trademark, the whole exercise was a bit of fun. Surely it wasn't going to be taken too seriously if a player inadvertently stepped out of line?

'All games need rules that are properly observed, otherwise all you get is chaos,' Rebecca pointed out mildly.

'Sure,' Jon agreed. 'That's why we'll do our best to conform.'

After stripping off their tracksuits the boys said they needed to limber up for a few minutes. Although they were supposed to be getting on with their own practising the girls tended to stand around and watch what was going on. After all, they might spot something that would be to their advantage in the match. Inevitably, Karen was more interested in the boys' physical appearance than their ability to pass and shoot.

'I rather like *him*,' she told Zoe, pointing to a dark-haired giant with shoulders as broad as a door.

'I expect he'll like you, later on,' replied Zoe, well aware of what to expect where Springholm's Goalkeeper was concerned. 'But if he's an attacker you'd better not let him get away with anything, otherwise

Julie will be really mad.'

Julie was busy conferring with Carrie. To make it a family double, as Rebecca put it, Carolyn had also been made captain of her side. Julie had no objection. In fact, she told Rebecca she thought it would work well because then Carolyn would be more involved with the game. That was just what Rebecca expected, too.

'Jon and I will be equally determined to win, you know,' Carolyn was emphasising. 'I would hate it if he came home boasting about how his team had beaten the pants off us, if you see what I mean.'

Julie did and they both giggled.

'Right,' Rebecca yelled loudly, and then remembered she had a whistle so she blew that as well. 'I think it's time we started. Can we have the non-players off the court, please?'

With unexpected gallantry, the Bouncers had invited the Shooters to start the game. Rebecca would have liked to insist that all the players shook hands with each other before the start but if it wasn't done naturally it was better not done at all. She was still apprehensive about the way in which the match would be played because she feared that the boys would either fool about or simply injure someone because of their clumsiness in an unfamiliar game.

Tara Morton, delighted to have another chance to

impress as Springholm's Centre, drew Carolyn into the attack from the outset. The boys seemed to make only half-hearted attempts to intercept before the ball reached Keeley. Springholm's Goal-attack was equally determined to keep her place in the side and, very deftly, she ducked away from a challenge and sent an underarm pass to Julie. It was a ploy they had practised during the week and it worked magically.

Julie, running across the width of the shooting circle as the ball reached her, stopped dead, pivoted and then, one-handed, lobbed the ball perfectly through the ring. Even by senior standards it was a brilliant goal, one of the best Julie had scored.

Brockwood's defenders had scarcely moved in an effort to prevent it but that by no means devalued the goal. Linton McCloud, who was Goalkeeper, looked bemused; then he laughed as if to show that he hadn't been bothering to defend anyway.

'Bit wasted on them, that goal,' Julie murmured to Carolyn, who was signalling her pleasure at the score.

'Never mind, they all count, and now the Bouncers must know they're in for a real game,' Keeley said as she congratulated Julie. 'Let's get another as fast as we can.'

It didn't take long. Vastly encouraged by starting

so well, Springholm kept possession when next they had the ball. It came to them, almost inevitably, because of an offence, a foot offence, committed by Jon Peachey himself who acknowledged his error with a raised hand to the umpire. But it was a costly mistake. Tara flung the ball to Carolyn, who'd been weaving all over the goal third, trying to open up Brockwood's defence. Keeley, operating on the opposite wing, took the ball on a finger-tip, knocked it up, caught it and threw it back to Carolyn – who promptly returned it to her. It was exactly the sort of ploy to irritate opponents, and the Bouncers were duly irritated. When, moments later, the attack was switched into the shooting circle Keeley was barged off the ball by Linton McCloud. Although he apologised immediately, it didn't sound genuine.

Rebecca, of course, was in no moral position to chastise the offender for his manner; she could only punish him according to the rules. Keeley herself took the penalty and her aim was perfect. The ball dropped through the net – and the Shooters were leading 2–0.

'Come on, lads, let's get stuck in,' Jon Peachey yelled. 'We're not concentrating.'

'Goodness,' remarked Carrie, 'I've never heard him shout like that before. Maybe they'll make him the regular captain after this.'

'Not if his team gets a thrashing from us,' Julie remarked. 'They'll probably ban him for life for that!'

Almost at once it was plain that the boys were beginning to concentrate, to ignore their basketball instincts and think about how best to play netball. Some of the very minor infringements they committed Rebecca tended to overlook; she recognised they weren't important in the context of the game. There was no point in unduly penalising the Brockwood players.

Jon Peachey, playing Centre, had more idea than most of his team-mates on how to control play and initiate attacks. It was he who provided the pass which brought the first real scoring chance for Brockwood. The ball was snapped up by the dark-haired giant Karen admired. To her delight he was the Bouncers' Goal-shooter. Now he ducked and weaved in the shooting circle as Karen, in playing terms, tried to put him off his shot. It was obvious, though, that he knew more than just the rudiments of the game. Waiting for an opponent's wobble, as any experienced netball player would, he aimed for the net as soon as he saw an opening. The ball disappeared through the ring as if drawn by a magnet. The Bouncers had pulled one back and they congratulated themselves.

'Good shot, Ben,' Karen remarked to the scorer with a breath-catching smile.

She would never have praised a female opponent. But, true to her nature, she had not only discovered the boy's name by listening to the Bouncers' calls; she was also letting him know she was aware of him as a person, not just as a player.

That goal acted as a stimulus to Springholm as well as to the scorers. Springholm sensed they were now being taken seriously. The two goals they had scored were genuine because Brockwood were showing they wanted to fight back.

The pace quickened perceptibly.

Julie was enjoying herself. So was Carrie, especially when she succeeded in by-passing her brother with a pass or outwitting him through a decoy movement in which Julie shared. Keeley, however, was not having a good time. Her partnership with Julie succeeded only spasmodically and she was finding it difficult to shake off the attentions of Linton McCloud. As she'd feared, he seemed to be concentrating all his attention on her when Springholm attacked. He was leaving Julie to be covered by his Goal-defence.

Linton didn't actually say anything to her (or nothing that she heard). But she knew he was eyeing her all the time: eyeing her in a distinctly unpleasant way. She knew she couldn't easily get round him or shoot past him because of his height. In any case, her own shooting was still not particularly skilful. Linton's presence had begun to unnerve her even before he touched her for the first time.

It happened when they both went up for a high ball that bounced from the post and ricocheted upwards. There was no real hope of Keeley reaching it ahead of Linton but she didn't let that deter her. Everything happened with such speed that Rebecca hadn't a chance of seeing the punch. In any case, McCloud was a soccer goalkeeper who knew very well how to get away with assaulting an opponent in the penalty area. He chose his target with care when Keeley's body was still airborne and shielding him from even the most acute umpire's gaze. His fist savagely buried itself in Keeley's kidney region. It travelled only a short distance but power was there.

Keeley was stumbling to her knees as the pain flared. Her gasp of mingled surprise and anguish wasn't loud. No one who heard it thought much of it. Players were always stumbling or tumbling even on a netball court where physical contact was barred and therefore wasn't supposed to occur. By the time she regained her balance and put her hand to her aching back the ball was being cleared and Linton

McCloud was outside the shooting circle, apparently shadowing Julie.

Keeley found she could hardly walk; the pain pulled her down with every step she took. Although she naturally hadn't seen the blow she could imagine just how it had happened. The punch was exactly the sort that Sandra had got away with time and time again. Sandra must have passed on to him details of her technique for terrorising her.

'You all right?' Rebecca inquired anxiously a few moments later when play had again swung towards Springholm's goal third.

'I – will – be,' Keeley replied through clenched teeth.

The pain was receding but it still wasn't easy to walk properly, let alone run. Yet she didn't want to go off. Until Linton hit her she'd been trying to enjoy the match. She knew that this time she wasn't going to give in to violence or run away. If it happened again, she was going to retaliate, whatever the consequences. In her eyes, this was no friendly match. It was a test of survival.

'Come on, Kee, you're slacking,' Julie shouted when she fumbled a pass.

Carolyn, now always in sympathy with Julie's attitudes, wrinkled her nose and looked significantly towards the side of the court where a substitute would normally be waiting. On this occasion, however, Springholm had no extra players to call on apart from Rebecca.

The boys were now playing more skilfully and the speed of their play was causing Karen and Zoe a lot of problems, some of their own making. Karen was indulging in banter with Ben. So she wasn't prepared for his sudden change of mood. When a team-mate hurled the ball from the other side of the court and yelled: 'Go, go, go!' Ben went. He went so swiftly he left her standing. Collecting the ball easily he flipped it through the ring with seemingly effortless accuracy for Brockwood's equaliser.

'Concentrate, Karen, concentrate!' Carolyn yelled at her Goalkeeper.

Karen had the grace to acknowledge her error with a wave of the hand. She didn't want Springholm to lose, however friendly she might become with Ben.

It had been agreed that the match would be fifteen minutes each way. At half-time both teams felt that was quite long enough, though for different reasons. Neither side was in any way confident of victory; both thought that if they lost at least they would lose with credit.

'Are you sure you're O.K.?' Rebecca inquired of

Keeley, who had spent the interval holding her back.

'Oh yes, I'm fine. Rarin' to go, in fact.'

She looked white but determined. Rebecca was half-convinced she should take her place but she feared the boys might not accept another umpire. So far the Bouncers had played the game according to the rules, and her rulings. With someone else in charge they might start to seize unfair advantages. She wished she had thought to bring some refreshments to share all round. That alone would have improved the atmosphere for undoubtedly some of the players looked tense. Even if she had, she suspected the teams would have remained apart during the break. Karen kept exchanging glances with Ben but that was as far as their ripening friendship went for the present. Linton was deliberately avoiding Keeley's gaze.

The match resumed at a frantic pace. Offences began to multiply rapidly. Offside was a constant problem for the boys and, much to their disgust, they had to surrender the ball frequently. Incidents of players grabbing the ball simultaneously also increased and at the toss-up it was noticeable that invariably the boys gained possession. It occurred to Rebecca that perhaps their speed of thought, of physical reaction, was the greater.

Then, in sudden, sharp contrast Julie moved decisively first to seize the initiative at a toss-up almost on the goal third line. As if by instinct, she whipped the ball backwards to Carolyn, who took it so sweetly she might have been expecting it. The boys were simply taken by surprise as Julie, sprinting into the shooting circle with remarkable acceleration, took the return pass high above her head. With the Brockwood defenders seemingly concentrating on Keeley in anticipation of a pass, Julie had what amounted to a free shot. And she was too skilful a player to miss that sort of chance. Unerringly the ball passed through the ring without touching the metal.

Springholm Shooters had regained the lead in exhilarating fashion. Julie received a cascade of congratulations from her team-mates. Even Ben was nodding with muted approval. After all, it was the sort of goal he'd have been proud to score himself.

Naturally, the boys were eager, almost desperate, to get back on level terms. But sheer strength and height were not enough. The girls were now playing as well as Rebecca had ever seen them play. The form of Carolyn Peachey was a revelation: she seemed incapable of putting a foot, or a hand, wrong. Rebecca experienced a pang of envy at the service Julie was receiving from the Wing-attack.

Keeley, too, was moving and throwing with rare determination. She couldn't, though, throw off the close attentions of the Goalkeeper. It was obvious to Rebecca he wasn't allowing Keeley so much as a centimetre of leeway inside or even outside the shooting circle. Carolyn had spotted that, too, and that's why she was intent on feeding Julie whenever possible. Another goal by Julie might just clinch the outcome of the match.

By now one or two spectators had materialised, though no one seemed to be taking sides. Some seemed simply mesmerised by the spectacle of boys playing girls at netball. Occasionally a watcher applauded a good catch or an astute pass.

The players began to appreciate an audience and one or two played up to them. Zoe surprised herself by intercepting a pass intended for Ben and instantaneously transferring the ball to Tara. That earned a burst of clapping and Zoe practically blushed. No one had taken notice of her like that before this match. Immediately she began to play better. She was one of the reasons why the boys failed to get an equaliser. Zoe and Springholm's Wing-defence missed nothing which might check the Bouncers' attack. At the other end Keeley strove to set up chances for her team-mate. But she could make no progress without the ball. Carrie was still using her only as a decoy.

Then, just as Carrie hurled a pass to the far limit of the shooting circle, Keeley, anticipating the direction brilliantly, charged across to receive it. Inevitably, Linton went with her, though her speed off the mark had given her a clear start. By the time she rose for the ball, however, he had caught up. She and Julie jumped together with Linton beside, and slightly behind, them. Julie, with her ability to climb high, was the first to touch the ball. She

touched it with her right hand but it fell away before she could secure it.

Keeley, twisting in mid-air in an effort to make the catch, was bumped by Linton. Whether it was deliberate or, for once, accidental, she didn't know. She fell sideways as she struck the ground – and then yelled with pain as Linton's foot landed on her thigh. Off-balance, he toppled backwards. As he scrambled to his feet beside her Keeley reacted fiercely and deliberately. Her right fist rocketed upwards, catching him under the jaw.

Linton's head snapped back and struck the floor with a resounding crack. A tremor seemed to run through his entire frame. Then he lay motionless.

Eight

For some moments hardly anyone moved at all. Keeley looked as stunned by what she had done as her victim did. Rebecca was the first to take action. Swiftly she reached his side, knelt and turned him on to his front with his head to one side and cradled in the crook of his arm. Then she stooped to listen to his breathing and take his pulse.

'How – how is he?' asked Jon Peachey, kneeling beside her.

'Concussed, probably,' Rebecca replied crisply. 'That's what usually happens when anybody gets a bang on the head like that and passes out. It depends –'

She stopped because Linton's eyelids were fluttering open. For a moment he looked utterly mystified and it was obvious he didn't know where he was or why he was lying on the floor. Then, beginning to recover, he sat up and stared at Jon and Rebecca.

'What's going on?' he asked, his voice sounding a little hoarse.

'You fell and banged your head,' Rebecca told him as she leaned forward to peer closely at his pupils. 'How do you feel now?'

Linton tried to shake his head, as if to clear it, but winced as he did so.

'Well, a bit woozy, actually,' he admitted. 'Look, did somebody hit me or something? I'm sure I felt something as I went down – I remember that.'

Most of the bystanders exchanged looks with Keeley but nobody seemed willing to tell Linton that he had been floored by an uppercut from Springholm's Goal-attack. Keeley herself, still looking stricken, felt it better to remain silent for the moment.

'Please look straight at me and watch my finger,' Rebecca said to Linton, holding up her right index finger and then moving it slowly and very deliberately from side to side. 'Now, can you follow that all right? Yes, it looks as if you can, your eyes are moving normally. Good.'

'Hey, what is this?' Linton demanded in his usual voice, although he now sounded slightly anxious.

'Don't worry,' Julie said in a reassuring manner. 'Rebecca knows what she's doing. She's had good training because she's in the Red Cross. So –'

'So what's that got to do with anything?' Linton cut in. His own aggression was plainly returning.

'It means that I understand something about injuries,' Rebecca told him with a smile. 'The Red Cross was founded to assist wounded soldiers on the battlefield. That's really what I'm doing now. But you seem to be recovering quite quickly.'

'Of course I am!' the Goalkeeper declared, springing to his feet as if to prove his fitness. But the effect was spoiled when he stumbled slightly and nearly fell again.

Rebecca, too, got to her feet and then went across to have a word with Brockwood's captain.

'Look, Jon,' she said quietly, 'I don't think Linton should take any further part in this match. He needs to rest and he needs to be watched to see that all is well. I believe he has mild concussion. It'll probably clear up as long as he doesn't exert himself in any way for the next hour or so. Probably he won't take that advice from me but I hope he will from you. If he does have any symptoms, if he's sick or sees double, he must see a doctor right away. Please tell him that.'

Jon nodded. 'O.K., if you think that's for the best. Linton's not going to like it but that can't be helped. I'm the skipper so he'll have to follow orders. Only trouble is, we don't have anyone else who can take over as Goalkeeper. So I think we'd better call the match off right now. What do you think, Carrie?'

His sister, who had just joined them, agreed. She had sensed that the injury to Linton, and what had led to it, had completely changed the atmosphere of the match. The excitement and the keenness to win had evaporated; nearly every player on both sides looked downcast. Even Karen and Ben were no longer looking at each other. Linton himself was still rubbing his head and muttering darkly to a team-mate. Like everyone else, he appeared to be ignoring Keeley. And she, although looking pale and upset, still had about her an air of defiance.

'I was very nearly ready to blow up for full-time,' Rebecca added. 'So we haven't really lost much playing time. And we did appreciate your playing us – you gave us some terrific challenges and that's bound to be good for our game overall. I'm just sorry it ended the way it did.'

'Well, these things happen in sport,' Jon said philosophically. 'Can't be helped. Linton will understand when he's calmed down. I'll have a word with Sandra, his girl-friend, and tell her to watch him closely. She won't object to that! They're always together, you know.'

Keeley, who had been edging towards them, heard what was being said. Suddenly she stepped forward and said fiercely to Jon: 'Don't forget to tell her who hit him and knocked him out. He deserved it for what he was trying to do to me. She'll know why I did it, Sandra will. Just tell her I've stopped being a victim. Tell her if I have to do the same to her, I will.'

Then she swung round and marched off towards the changing-rooms. No one attempted to stop her, not even Linton McCloud.

'What was all that about?' Jon asked the girls.

'Tell you later,' his sister replied. 'I only know bits of the story but I can guess some of the rest. I don't think she'll make a habit of knocking people out.'

'Well, I must say, she certainly packs a punch,' Jon remarked half-admiringly. 'Linton's a tough guy to tangle with but your girl definitely came off best there. Right, then, we'll pack it in. See you around.'

The players who were still on the court shook hands before everyone drifted off to the changing-rooms. Jon had his arm round Linton's shoulders and was talking to him very earnestly. To Rebecca's relief, Linton appeared to be listening calmly. She still had a marginal fear that he would seek his revenge on Keeley, even though he claimed not to know what had happpened to him.

Most of the girls were clustered around Keeley when Rebecca and Carolyn returned to their changing-room. They were firing questions which Keeley either laughed aside or refused to answer. Why had Linton been picking on her? How had she learned to punch like that? Who was Sandra? Zoe thought Keeley had been very brave to go for someone who had been tormenting her when he was much bigger and heavier. Karen, fairly predictably, took a different view: she felt that Keeley's action

105

had simply ruined the game. After this, they'd never find another boys' team willing to play them at anything.

By now it was obvious that Keeley didn't mind being the centre of attention but she still wasn't giving much away about her motives. Eventually her team-mates gave up asking her and went off for a shower or got changed. They had plenty to talk about among themselves.

Keeley herself was in no hurry to leave. Patiently she waited until the last pair, Julie and Carrie, had left and Rebecca was the only other girl in the changing-room. So far Rebecca, although giving her the occasional wan smile, hadn't asked for an explanation of her conduct. As the captain of Springholm, she was entitled to demand one, as Keeley was well aware.

'Look, Rebecca, I'm sorry that I broke up the game,' she said as soon as they were alone, 'but, honestly, I'm not sorry for what I did. You know, when he jumped on my leg he was deliberately trying to hurt me, *really* hurt me. He'd managed it once before already though he was clever enough to make sure you didn't see the incident. So he only got what he deserved. And you said yourself, it's only mild concussion. He'll be over it in no time.'

Rebecca nodded. 'Yes, I'm sure all that's true,

Kee. But there was more to it than that, wasn't there? I didn't realise that Sandra was involved until you mentioned her. Then I asked around among the boys and discovered Linton's her boy-friend. I gather the reason why no one retaliated on Linton's behalf was because everyone realised that you two were caught up in a private feud. I think we're lucky the boys did take it all so well. But we can't have that sort of thing happening again. We can't have private *wars* breaking out on the court.'

Keeley put her hand on Rebecca's arm. 'It won't happen again, Becky, I swear it won't. You see, I know how to deal with the Sandra problem now. I've solved it.'

'*How* can you be sure?'

'It was something Carrie said when she lent me the boxing gloves. She said they give you confidence just to put them on. Well, that's true. I have felt confident. Whenever I see Sandra again I'll be able to tackle her head on. Even if she hasn't got the message via Linton, she'll see for herself in future that I can stand up for myself. She can't scare me any more so she'll give up trying.'

She paused and then added with a grin: 'Anyway, I'm really a peace-loving sort of person so there won't be anybody else, boy or girl, I want to have a crack at! My boxing days are over. I'm giving Carrie the gloves back.'

'I'm glad to hear it,' Rebecca said, smiling. 'I don't want to have to deal with any more battlefield injuries. But I'd like to know what started all this. I can promise you, Kee, I won't be telling anyone else. No, not anyone at all.'

Keeley barely hesitated. 'Yes, I believe that, Becky, because we're true friends now, you and I. You've been really very kind to me. Well, Sandra and I were the best of mates, but in a different sort of way. We spent a lot of time together mostly because we didn't have anything else to do, any other hobbies or things like that. A lot of the time we used to drift around the shops, especially the big stores, trying on clothes and spraying on free perfume and generally having a laugh. Well, then I discovered Sandra was shoplifting, pinching all sorts of things, things she didn't even want, some stuff she didn't even *like*.'

She bit her lip and seemed uncertain what to say next. But Rebecca didn't interrupt. A moment or two later Keeley resumed her story.

'She was good at it, so good that I didn't even know she was doing it until she told me. Yet I'd actually been standing beside her at one counter when she nicked a fountain pen, a really lovely new model in mixed, streaky colours. After that, I didn't want to have anything to do with her. I hate the idea of stealing. Well, the following Saturday, when she was on her own, the store detective caught her at it. But she managed to convince him it was her first time and so he let her off, saying they'd prosecute if she ever did it again.'

Keeley sighed. 'Of course, I expect you can guess the rest, Becky. Sandra swore that I must have informed on her, must have warned the store to look out for her. But I never did! I wouldn't rat on a friend, and she had been a friend. Then she started attacking me, saying that if ever it got out that she'd been threatened with prosecution she'd make certain I suffered more than she did. Like a fool, I didn't hit back. I just tried to avoid her; but she's often found a way of ambushing me and, well, just being rotten. But now that I've proved I can stand up to her boy-friend, even clobber him for good measure, I think I can handle anything she tries in the future.'

'Is she still shoplifting, do you think?'

'I doubt it. The store detective really scared her. She's terrified of her parents so she knows what'd happen if they ever found out. And, anyway, all her spare time these days is spent with Linton.'

Decisively, Rebecca stood up. 'Well, as you say, Kee, it should all be settled now and so you can concentrate on your netball without worrying too much about what the opposition are going to do to you. I must say, it seemed to me that when you were angry – before you actually knocked Linton out – you were playing as well as I've ever seen you play. Maybe you play better when your temper's up. Some players do. But with others bad temper simply causes their game to disintegrate.'

'So, Becky, do you think I stand a chance of playing again even when you and Julie are back together as the shooters?' Keeley asked tentatively as they headed for the door. 'I mean, after what happened you might –'

'Oh yes, I should think so,' Rebecca replied with a grin. She put her arm round Keeley's shoulders. 'After all, I don't think we should change a winning team.'

'A *winning* team?' Keeley was perplexed.

'Yes. Hadn't you realised? We did *beat* the boys, you know, by 3–2. That's one reason why I didn't mind finishing the match there and then after your K.O. punch. It must be good for our morale to know we defeated a team of boys who were bigger and heavier than us and who were just as keen – keener if anything – to win. I reckon the Shooters can be proud of this victory. So we must make the most of it.'

Nine

With the ball on the palm of her hand, Julie France was writing her name in the air. Then she tossed the ball upwards, caught it on her finger-tips and twirled it round and round. Spectators, believing that this was something of a juggling display put on for their entertainment, applauded.

The clapping took her by surprise but Julie was too much of an extrovert not to respond: so with the ball still balanced on one horizontal hand, she curtseyed neatly to the crowd, and duly received another ovation. In fact, all she'd been doing originally was practising her ball control. One of her favourite tricks was to put her hand on top of the ball and hold it nonchalantly with outstretched fingers. Now, as the moments ticked away to the start of the Manor House Cup Final, Julie wanted to make sure that all her skills were, literally, on hand.

On the opposite side of the court Rebecca and

Karen Honley were involved in some furious, and very hard, catching practice. The entire Springholm team had come out early to warm-up before what every one of them regarded as the most important match of their lives. None of them had ever played in a Cup Final before and they were determined to make the most of the occasion. Karen had echoed the desires of all of them when she declared before leaving the changing-room: 'It'll be the happiest moment of my life if I get my hands on a winner's medal. Nobody'll ever be able to take that away from me!'

After the first round scare against Netherlee they'd made remarkably smooth progress to the Final. The later stages of the competition were played during a weekend on a secondary school court and in the semi-final they'd had a huge slice of luck. With the scores level in the last seconds of the game, Springholm had been awarded a penalty in rather dubious circumstances. In spite of the tension all around her, Julie had been as nerveless as ever: her shot was perfect and the scorer was turning round to embrace Carolyn even before the ball cleared the net.

Their opponents, Tolworth, had reached the Final with some easy victories over relatively poor teams and so they'd had luck on their side, too.

Now, as they marched on to the court in formation, spectacularly attired in orange and light blue, there was enthusiastic applause from their large band of supporters.

'So that's Tiona Abbey, is it?' Karen remarked, pointing out the towering figure of Tolworth's Goal-shooter and captain. 'Well, she's not going to get any shots past me today, however good she's supposed to be.'

'Funny name,' remarked Zoe. 'What's it mean?'

'Somebody told me it means Cornish Princess,' Carolyn grinned. 'That must be why she has such a regal air!'

'Sounds more like a public monument to me,' sniffed Karen. 'She's as tall as one anyway.'

Tiona certainly displayed a calculatedly formal manner as she introduced her team to a local author, who was to present the trophy and the medals. She condescended to shake hands with her rival captain, Rebecca, but there wasn't a glimmer of a smile as she did so. Nor did she respond to Rebecca's polite good wishes.

Tolworth's other star player was their Centre, Magdalena Axwood, lithe and dark-haired with brooding eyes. On Julie's advice, Magdalena was to be shadowed by her opposite number, Tara Morton, leaving Carrie free to initiate Springholm's attacks.

Keeley had been slotted into the team at Wing-defence and, in recent matches, had more than earned her place. Initially, she hadn't been keen on playing in defence but now, as she'd confessed to Becky, she was quite revelling in the role. Her experience as a temporary stand-in for Julie and then Rebecca herself had given her an insight into how attackers operated; so she was well placed to anticipate and defeat their moves.

The umpire made a point of telling both teams that the rules would be rigorously enforced (none of the players had expected anything else) and that any attempts at gamesmanship would be severely punished. Hardly anyone knew what she was getting at but Rebecca suspected the umpire was simply saying something that sounded significant because it was expected of her at a Cup Final.

Play was very tentative in the opening stages. Passes were fumbled and even dropped. One spectator yelled, 'Come on, you can do better than this!' and all who heard her agreed, including the players. The first shot at goal was attempted by Tiona but Karen's well-timed jump helped her to deflect the ball. Magdalena was seeing very little of the ball because of Tara's close attentions and one outstanding interception. So there seemed to be something of a stalemate in the centre third.

Julie was constantly on the move, darting between opponents in order to unsettle them even when there was no likelihood of the ball reaching her. Tolworth's Goalkeeper had her own ritual: she was never still for a moment, dancing to one side, then to the other, and performing what was akin to a ballet routine whenever Rebecca moved into what she plainly regarded as her personal territory. Yet the upper part of her body was rigid as a vertical ironing-board.

Carrie was the player who broke the deadlock. Following a rush to reach a high pass Rebecca wasn't able to check her progress before stepping out of court while holding the ball; but, as she tilted over the line, she flung the ball backwards in the hope that it would be caught by one of her own team-mates. Even if it wasn't, the ball would still have gone to the opposition because she'd taken it out of court. Because this ploy had been practised time and again by the Springholm players Carrie had leapt forward to seize the ball, spin and then fling it with perfect timing and accuracy to Julie, hovering on the edge of the shooting circle.

With the Goalkeeper out of range because she was really concerned only with what Rebecca was up to, and the Goal-defence suddenly caught flat-footed, Julie's one jump took her into the circle – and there was no one at all to challenge her. From that distance and angle the shot was a hard one. But the difficult shots were the focus of much of her training.

The ball rimmed the goal before dropping through – and Springholm Shooters were in the lead.

Keeley, with some dour defence, and Karen, athletic in everything she did, kept opponents at bay when Tolworth tried to step up their game after that setback. So far Magdalena hadn't been free to set up a single attacking move because of Tara's vigilance. Ceaselessly, though, she was seeking an opening; and it came in the form of a very fast underarm pass that took Tara by surprise.

Magdalena rapidly exchanged passes with her Wing-attack and managed to reach the perimeter of the shooting circle. Tiona was in the far corner, isolated because she had deliberately stepped as far back as possible, and she took the pass at the very extent of her reach. Her shot was the equal of anything Julie had achieved in recent matches; its parabola took it clean through the net.

Tolworth's supporters were suddenly delirious. They had seen two goals of the highest quality: but the second was the only one that mattered to them. They could sense that the worse moments for their colourfully-clad team were over. The orange sun was shining brightly.

That began a period of ascendancy for Tolworth. For what seemed liked minutes on end, they swarmed round the shooting circle and shots peppered the post. Inevitably, one had to go in. With an unselfish reverse pass Tiona gave her Goal-attack an opening and with an easy flip the ball passed through the net.

'Come on, Shooters, come ON!' Julie, fists clenched, called to her team-mates. 'We're letting it slip away.'

Rebecca looked at her and gave a slight shake of the head. She always felt it unwise to show much emotion just because your team had gone one goal down.

Then, with the first interval almost due, Springholm drew level. Once again Carrie was the spring of invention. When the ball came to her from Julie she knocked it upwards, sprang to catch it and then, all in the same flowing movement, hurled a pass to Rebecca on the far side of the court. That manoeuvre completely outwitted two opponents: the one who'd been marking Carrie herself and the one waiting for what she was sure was the predictable pass to Julie.

Rebecca, darting forward, bounced a low pass

117

between two defenders on the edge of the circle straight into Julie's arms. Julie returned it instantaneously. Rebecca's guardian, the balletic Goalkeeper, was utterly confused by the bounced pass and she hadn't recovered when, one-handed, Rebecca tossed the ball through the ring. Julie, after embracing the scorer, turned to hug Carrie.

'Great pass, Carrie, oh great pass!' she said ecstatically.

118

Rebecca didn't say so to anyone but the low, bounced pass was a trick she had picked up from the match with the boys. They'd employed it most effectively more than once and Rebecca had been waiting for the ideal opportunity to try it out. She doubted if they'd get away with it again in this game; Tolworth's skipper possessed just as much tactical awareness as Julie. During the break she'd be ordering her defenders to be alert for that move again. If the element of surprise was missing then the pass wouldn't be so successful.

'Do you think we should make any changes?' Julie inquired as all the players took a breather.

Rebecca shook her head. 'I can't see any need. Everyone's playing pretty well and trying hard. We've just got to be patient and keep probing for openings. That policy worked well against Swanhaven – oh, and Netherlee, too, if it comes to that.'

After the resumption the game changed quite dramatically for in the space of two minutes there was a flurry of scoring, with two goals to each side. Both of Springholm's were converted by Julie as a result of the Goalkeeper's obsession with marking Rebecca, leaving Julie to be marshalled by the less efficient Goal-defence. After Julie's second successful shot Tiona stalked across to speak forcefully to her defenders.

The greatest danger now to Springholm's own defence was created by Magdalena. She'd realised that she could out-jump Tara and somehow had conveyed to her team-mates that when they passed to her the ball must be sent high. But she also had the subtlety to vary her own distribution by favouring now the fast underarm, and then the high overhead, pass. Tara was beginning to look flustered and frustrated. And, inevitably, the ball was going more and more often to Magdalena, as if drawn by a magnet. Yet, in spite of her best efforts, Tolworth still couldn't pull ahead again and at the final whistle the scores were level. In the dying seconds the pace had been so hectic, the chances so very, very close to success for both sides, that nearly all the players looked completely drained when that whistle sounded.

They knew, though, that extra time would have to be played: three minutes each way.

'We'd never forgive ourselves if we lost now,' Rebecca told her team. She knew that nothing else needed to be said to motivate them. Team spirit had never been higher.

She had, though, decided on a tactical switch: Tara and Keeley were to change places. Tara seemed relieved that she was to have a freer role from now on while Keeley showed pleasure at being asked to clamp down on Magdalena's activities. Rebecca was banking on Keeley's speed and resourcefulness being vital factors. In recent weeks the red-haired girl's determination to lose weight and improve her mobility had quite obviously paid off. On top of that, her confidence in her game had soared since becoming a regular member of Springholm's defence.

The break was brief. Remarkably, no one had suffered any strains or sprains despite the fierce pace of the game; and no substitutes were called upon. Those who started the match would finish it.

Then, for the first time, Springholm took the lead and kept it for longer than two minutes. The goal was a direct result of a 'wall' push by Carrie almost on the line of the shooting circle: instead of catching the ball when it was passed to her by Tara, she deflected it with both palms towards Julie. That trick confused two defenders but not Julie, who had worked it out with Carrie in training. The Springholm Goal-attack scooped the ball up and popped it neatly through the ring.

Some spectators thought the whole thing was a fluke; others, more knowledgeable, recognised the inherent skills of the players who had constructed and completed the move.

'Three minutes. That's all we've got to hold out for, and the Cup is ours,' Rebecca reminded her players at the change-over.

'We'll do it, we'll do it,' Julie exclaimed, as much to herself as to anyone. But they didn't.

Midway through the last period of extra time Tolworth, still attacking with verve and intelligence and not for a moment succumbing to nerves, drew level yet again. This time, though, it was through a Springholm error: in trying to jump too high and too far for an interception Karen Honley lost her balance and sprawled on the edge of the court. Tiona, who collected the ball, thus had the simplest of shots: and she didn't miss those.

Karen looked devastated and Rebecca was quick to absolve her of any blame.

'It could happen to anyone,' she pointed out. 'And you've already prevented a dozen goals. Forget it, Karen. We're still in the game.'

But Karen, thinking only of the medal she wanted so desperately, couldn't speak. She was on the verge of tears. Yet, when Tolworth attacked again moments later, she turned the ball away from Tiona's eager hands quite brilliantly. Springholm hadn't really lost their composure after all. When the end of extra time was signalled they were the ones pressing for the decisive score.

'What happens now?' was what everyone was asking and even the umpire appeared not to know. Hastily she was consulting other officials and representatives of both teams. So far as anyone could recall this situation hadn't arisen before; and it seemed dreadfully unfair to contemplate playing another match on another day.

'It has to be sudden death – the first team to score another goal,' the umpire announced. 'That goal will end the game and decide the winners.'

'Sudden death!' echoed Keeley. 'Goodness, that sounds ominous.'

It was the quality of play that was bad when the match resumed once more; but that was hardly a surprise. Passes were dropped and players bumped into each other, simply because no one dared to make a mistake. The first chance of a score fell to Tolworth and for once in her life the clinical Tiona muffed it. Springholm breathed again as Tolworth's supporters uttered a deep, collective groan.

Play switched to the other end. And, on the perimeter of the circle, Keeley and Magdalena grabbed the ball simultaneously. It had to be, and was, a toss-up. Carrie was to take it for Springholm and in the second before she did Julie signalled to her from inside the circle, a signal that the Goalkeeper spotted.

In the fraction of a second that the ball was being sent upwards Carrie leapt and grabbed it; and, in the same movement, hurled it straight to Rebecca. For once Rebecca was isolated: her permanent shadow had chosen precisely the wrong moment to cover Julie instead. The signal had been misinterpreted, just as Julie hoped it might be.

Rebecca turned, aimed and with aplomb sent the ball on its way and through the ring for the goal that won the Manor House Cup for Springholm Shooters.

Julie, before the ball could touch the ground, was ecstatically leaping higher than she did when scoring.

'I learned that from the boys – they always watched the umpire's eyes before they moved,' she explained when she came down to earth. 'When they saw the umpire glancing upwards, they moved – because the ball was on its way. And it worked! That's zazzy, absolutely zazzy!'

She still had her arms round Rebecca and Carrie as the teams lined up for the presentation of the Cup and the coveted medals.